The Age of Magic

The Age of Magic

Ben Okri

W F HOWES LTD

This large print edition published in 2015 by
W F Howes Ltd
Unit 4, Rearsby Business Park, Gaddesby Lane,
Rearsby, Leicester LE7 4YH

1 3 5 7 9 10 8 6 4 2

First published in the United Kingdom in 2014
by Head of Zeus Ltd.

A CIP catalogue record for this book is available
from the British Library

ISBN 978 1 47129 603 1

Typeset by Palimpsest Book Production Limited,
Falkirk, Stirlingshire

)ound in Great Britain
al Ltd, Padstow, Cornwall

MIX
Paper from
responsible sources
FSC
www.fsc.org   FSC® C013056

A work of art that retraced the conquest of
happiness would be a revolutionary one.

Camus, *Noces* (1937)

The age of magic has begun.
Unveil your eyes.

Pensero, *Il Camino* (1321)

BOOK I

THE JOURNEY AS HOME

CHAPTER 1

Some things only become clear much later.

CHAPTER 2

They were on the train from Paris to Switzerland when the white mountains and the nursery rhythms of the wheels lulled him to sleep. He found himself talking to a Quylph.

'What are you afraid of?' it said.

'Why should I be afraid of anything?' Lao replied.

'Maybe you are afraid of Malasso?'

'Why should I be afraid of him?'

'Everyone else is.'

'I don't know him.'

'People are afraid of what they don't know.'

'Never met him. Why should I be scared of him?'

'You tell me.'

Lao became aware, out of the corner of his eyes, that everything seemed luminous. In a compartment full of businessmen, tourists, and young lovers the Quylph looked perfectly at ease. This bothered Lao.

'Then it must be life you are afraid of,' the Quylph said after a while.

There are some conversations so strange that they are only remembered much later, but not noticed at the time.

The Quylph, in a unique space, occupied the seat across from Lao. He felt lucky to see it.

With a hint of amusement, it said:

'Do you know what the luckiest thing is?'

'No.'

'It is to be at home everywhere.'

Outside the window the mountains changed from white to green.

'You may see me again later,' smiled the Quylph. 'But don't look out for me.'

'Wait! I want to ask you a question.'

'You had your chance,' the Quylph said with an expression at once malicious and droll. 'Be more awake next time.'

CHAPTER 3

Lao slept in a shining orb. He woke up at his table, with a book on his lap, and the world was different. The jagged mountains raced past the large window. Mistletoe was asleep with a smile on her face. At that moment Jim, the director of the documentary they were making, appeared in front of him.

'We need to film you interviewing your fellow passengers.'

Lao stared blankly at Jim's benign jowled face. He was still trying to decipher the inscription that was the Quylph and his hearing was slow.

'Are you all right?' Jim said.

'Fine! Great! When do you want me?'

'Whenever you're ready.'

'I'm ready now.'

It turned out that Jim wasn't. He had figured Lao would give him trouble for about thirty minutes, which would have given Sam, the cameraman, enough time to finish his shots at the other end of the train. Jim had expected Lao to be difficult, and was a little annoyed that he wasn't. On the whole, Lao thought, we don't like people changing on us. It means we have to change too, and we dislike making the effort. We prefer them predictable. Jim stood there not knowing what to do. Lao sat back down, and Mistletoe woke up.

'Come get me when you are ready,' Lao said.

'I'm ready,' said Mistletoe.

'Okay,' said Jim, leaving reluctantly.

'Not you,' Lao said, squeezing Mistletoe's hand.

CHAPTER 4

They were making a television documentary about a journey to Arcadia, in Greece. In those days seven people were needed to film such a journey. They had started in London and had filmed in Paris and were now bound for the Goetheanum in Basel, Switzerland. Along the way they were filming travellers, asking what their idea of Arcadia was, what their ideal of happiness might be. They were making a journey to a place, but in truth they were making a journey to an idea.

There were eight of them: seven involved in the filming, and Mistletoe, Lao's companion. The journey which began as a documentary became one in which, against their wills, they were being changed.

CHAPTER 5

While he was waiting, Lao began thinking of the persona he would adopt. He conceived of life as a game in which one gets to play many roles and have many personas. He thought it best not to be too hung up on consistency. Only the dead are consistent.

The imp of impersonation came over him. He thought about how the camera makes one fall in love with an image of oneself, and perpetuates a false reality. What if by sheer repetition we become the person we most often pretend to be? Does that mean there is no authentic self? Are we made of habits, compressed by time, like layered rocks?

These questions turned in his mind as he prepared to meet the travellers he was to interview. His mind was unclear.

CHAPTER 6

Husk, who was in charge of all logistics of filming, came over to fetch Lao. She was thin and efficient and neurotically beautiful in her floral dress. She had already scanned the passengers for suitable candidates. The four people she chose were white, middle-class, American, and were travelling together.

She considered that, of the four, the lady who spoke with confidence was the ideal person to speak for the group. Husk thought she had the most interesting personality. She explained all this to Lao while they were standing between compartments, and she had to raise her voice because of the grinding of the wheels.

'They're a lovely group. I've spoken to them all. Just be calm. Are you sure you're all right? You look as if you're not quite here. The lady called Barbara is definitely the leader. She's got great personality, as you'll see. Are you sure you're okay?'

From the beginning of the journey Husk had entertained doubts about Lao as the presenter of the film. She doubted he had the qualities required, doubted his grasp of the subject, and his character.

Lao was aware of this, and of his reputation for being difficult, and it amused him.

'I think so,' he replied.

'Just remember the one with personality,' she said.

CHAPTER 7

While they were waiting for Sam to set up the cameras, Lao thought about the nature of personality. He wondered how much of a role it played in the outcome of events. He wondered how much was possible, or failed to be possible, because of it. But what is personality, he asked himself? The general theory is that it is active, performed, and larger than life. But it seemed to him that personality is the outward presence of an inner accomplishment. It exerts its influence unseen, like the moon on the tide. It sways without knowing that it does. It is akin to talent or an innate gift. The strategies of Alexander, thought Lao, are a metaphor of his personality rather than of his calculation. History might be the story of personality acting on time and memory. Maybe, when we immerse ourselves in the genius of existence, Lao thought, personality can even overcome fate.

Sam sent word through Riley, his gamine assistant, that the cameras were ready, and that filming could begin. But what happened next taught Lao a significant lesson about what is generally called personality. He learned about the power of the silent ones.

CHAPTER 8

The film crew were ready for him; all seven of them were there in the compartment. The camera infused its drug into Lao's system. He tried to become a seducer of eyes. Love me and lie, he thought to the camera, as he went to meet the four Americans.

They were seated together at a table. The two women, Emily and Barbara, had the window seats. The men, Bob and Scott, were big clean-shaven fellows. Scott, Emily's husband, was facing the direction of travel. Bob was backing it. All four in their late fifties looked healthy and prosperous, and seemed reasonably pleased with their lives. They looked at Lao with expectant faces. Whom should I address, he thought, in a mild panic? Do I speak to all four as if they are one person? He decided to address them individually.

He told them about the journey so far, and engaged them in the small talk of all travellers. His idea was to enter the profound through the simple gate. He let them choose their own leader from among them, the one who had the most to say and said it well. The two men seemed friendly enough. They regarded him with an openness touched with scepticism, Bob apparently the more open of the two.

'Have you heard of Arcadia?' Lao asked them.

There was a curious silence as they digested the word.

CHAPTER 9

Lao noticed, for the first time, the architecture of the word. It began and ended with the first letter of the alphabet. Beginning with a beginning and ending with a beginning too. There was also a beginning right at its centre. It occurred to him that letters might be symbolic, might conceal deeper meanings. He glimpsed the word's hinterland.

Begin at the beginning; at the mid-point begin again; and at the end return to the beginning. Never move far from the alpha of life. Replenish yourself in the aleph. Renew the core with the alf. In A we begin and to A we return. Four rivers flow into the Garden of Eden. In one of them, as an old commentary says, *the gold of the land is good.* A fifth river can be said to flow from Eden to Arcadia, and its allegories are wonderful, its gold good. When we are young we set out with dreams. In the middle of the journey of our lives we find perhaps that we have lost our way. At the end we find the origin; and we begin again.

CHAPTER 10

Lao shook himself.

'Have you heard of Arcadia?'

Bob spoke first. He had a good face and an eye that distrusted salesmen.

'Well, Arcadia is where we've come from, and I've heard about the one you're travelling to,' he said.

Lao realized that they had been briefed by Husk, and this threw him a little.

'What does Arcadia mean to you?'

'I don't know.'

Jim, who had been following the conversation, came over and whispered something slowly in Lao's left ear, as if engaged in a serpent-like form of hypnotism. It made Lao uneasy. He told Lao to restate his theme for the camera's benefit. Lao, inwardly bristling, asked the group:

'Which is best, travelling or arriving?'

'Arriving,' said Bob.

'I'd say the travelling itself,' said Barbara. 'There's something new each day, a sense of anticipation about things you haven't seen before.'

'I think both,' said Scott, who worked in the US

17

Navy. 'It's interesting to see other cultures, see how other people live.'

The silent lady near the window hadn't spoken yet. She had a thoughtful smile, and a glow that emphasised her silence.

CHAPTER 11

Lao directed his next question to her. Still she didn't speak, but smiled tenderly. Barbara answered the question instead. There are those who want to be heard and there are the silent ones. Months later when all that seemed significant has been forgotten, the mysterious light on their faces lingers.

Lao asked another question.

'Do you think travelling is an escape?'

'Yes,' said Bob.

'An escape to what?'

'Sometimes to the past,' Barbara said.

'What's the value of escaping to the past?'

'It helps to understand what is happening today and where we are going in the future.'

Lao looked round at all four of them.

'The idea behind Arcadia,' he said, 'is the suspicion that we have lost something, the feeling that we tend to lose our best dreams. Take Atlantis . . .'

'Yeah,' said Scott with sudden passion, 'they always seem to lose it. Something keeps creeping in and they destroy themselves. Rome was the last lot.'

'Can we regain something of the golden ages?'

This brought from Bob a meditation on the golden years of peace under Emperor Augustus, in contrast to the wars of contemporary times.

'We enjoyed former Yugoslavia so much – Croatia, Slovenia, Bosnia, beautiful countries. In the lovely town of Mostar they have a bridge from the twelfth century and it was the most painted bridge in the world. And now it's gone because of the wars. Yesterday we were in Sainte-Chapelle and we read that it had been destroyed at one time or another and they keep reconstructing it. People want to stay in touch with their past, but things happen in history. So there's this continuous destruction and reconstruction.'

'Why do we keep losing our best dreams?'

'Greed mostly,' said Scott. 'Power and corruption. With corruption it starts a downward curve, then it falls apart, then we go back and start all over again. We never learn.'

With perverse timing Propr, the temperamental sound man, announced that the recording machine needed new batteries. He also wanted Lao and the Americans to speak more clearly. There seemed to him too much noise in the carriage all of a sudden. His delicate ears had picked up intrusions no one else had noticed. With his gangly frame and his comic moustache he fussed over the batteries. The passengers looked on with forbearance.

When the problem was fixed, Jim whispered in

Lao's left ear that he should move on to his key question.

An almost sacred stillness came over the crew as the filming began.

The nature of the conversation was about to change.

CHAPTER 12

'I want to ask you all what your personal Arcadia might be. What is your idea of a private paradise? Is it a place, a book, a person, a piece of music, a painting?' Lao asked them.

'I feel it is when we have our family together,' said Scott.

Bob was about to speak when an overlap began. Two voices in the same space. But the gentle one commanded the ear. The camera, lover of novelty, turned in the direction of the new voice.

Her silence had gathered all the missed opportunities of the conversation. She spoke without any special emphasis. She spoke not to be heard, but because things had reached their limit, and a little transcendence was needed. There is something poignant about having to use words when silence would be best. But the camera cannot transmit the wisdom of silence. The Bhagavad Gita says: *More blessed than a thousand words, is one word that brings peace.* The camera might reply: *If you want to touch the hearts and minds of millions, make it visible, speak the words. Then you can use the power of the devil to serve the sublime.*

CHAPTER 13

And so Emily, the silent one, from New York, an unsilent city, said:

'When we've been travelling around I've often thought: *Oh, this would be a good place to be,* and *that would be an excellent place to live.* And yet, after I've seen everything I've decided that home, wherever that may be, is the place for feelings of peace. And if I can be at peace with myself then that is the most important thing. I think travelling teaches one that. It teaches you that the grass may be greener on the other side, but that basically most of us are happiest wherever we feel at home.'

There is a moment in all endeavours when, after much effort, one comes upon something. At the beginning one may have imagined that what one is searching for is a castle or a mountain or a lump of fame. But one comes upon something truer and simpler. It is smaller than one imagined, but it is right and best for one. It is what the heart needs. This humble thing will do. That's how it was after the silent lady spoke.

The film crew knew that the camera had found what it sought.

CHAPTER 14

The train sped on past run-down houses on the edges of small towns. The interview was over. As Lao made his way back through the carriages to his seat, he fell into a stained-glass reverie inspired by the rhythm of the train.

The best thing about death is having lived fully, Lao thought. Lived richly the possibilities. The best thing about life is death. Going back home. Living teaches us that home is best. Home is where we never left, but only thought we had. But you have to live fully to know that. And you have to know where is truly home.

A train gliding
Into the dark light.
Oxen in the grass.
The fields singing.
A lost dream.

BOOK II

A LITTLE MEDITATION
ON EVILING

CHAPTER 1

It was only much later that Lao noticed the graffiti on the broken walls, the dust-covered vegetation, the families in ragged houses staring with pale eyes at the passing train.

It was only when he was sitting down that he realised what he had not been seeing. Mistletoe was drawing a long jagged wall, and the drawing brought the realisation to him. He became aware that he was living backwards. He was dimly conscious that he was rarely in the present moment, and that, as in a time-lapse, he was always arriving at the place he had been minutes or hours ago.

Maybe it was being on the journey, maybe it was having acres of time on his hands, but he found himself thinking in a way he hadn't done in a long time.

He saw how, in not living in the present, life was always slipping away from him. How could he catch up? It occurred to him that this was one of the benefits of illness: giving people time to catch up with themselves, to arrive at where they are in life's fast-moving story. But if the dislocation has become too entangled and confused, what is to be done? How do we disentangle? How do we stop living backwards, he wondered?

CHAPTER 2

Lao could have sworn that someone whispered into his ear that the inverse of the word live is evil. He had never noticed it before and it surprised him.

Without allowing himself to ponder what other revelations might be hidden in the inversion of words, he pursued the implication of the insight. If the opposite of live is evil then to die in life – that is evil. To live is to love, evolve, create. To live is to be replenished by the origins. Evil is exile from the water of life. Then, thought Lao, Arcadia is the place where life is renewed, where evil is turned around.

CHAPTER 3

Staring out of the window, Lao became gloomy. Where had it come from?

For a long time gloom had been his normal mode of being. It was an inseparable shadow.

But on this journey his gloominess had become less familiar, like an old shoe not worn for a long time. It still felt comfortable, but Lao was becoming comfortable with something else.

Then he realised that he had wandered away from the Arcadian mood awoken by the silent lady. Or maybe it was her glow that made him aware of his gloom.

Across from him Mistletoe was still drawing. She had that smile on her face.

Outside the window, urban ruins tumbled past his eyes. Maybe that was what had induced the gloominess. Then a shadow fell across him and a voice said:

The way you live depends on the pact you made with your spirit.

Lao leapt up and looked around. No one was there. Only the other passengers in their seats, reading newspapers or staring into the distance.

Lao sat down again and something, a passing presence, whispered the word *Malasso*. Lao looked around anxiously again. Mistletoe smiled.

'You fell asleep and something woke you and you jumped up suddenly. It's okay. Everything's fine.'

Lao stayed silent. He stared at the urban ruins. They seemed endless. Tenements and dilapidated buildings. Edges of towns in decomposition. He wondered why the worst aspects of cities were always visible from trains. He found himself paying more attention to the ugly sites they were passing through. He found himself eviling, reinventing the world in malice. He liked nothing that he saw. He tried not to look at Mistletoe. In that mood she would be re-made in his eviling. She must have sensed this for she got up and quietly went away.

CHAPTER 4

The rest of the film crew were coming through the carriage, busy with shot sequences. Sam, with a hand-held camera, was taking close-ups of people's faces. Riley, Sam's assistant, was just behind him, holding canisters, ready to change the film when required. Lao stared at them, eviling.

Sam loved focusing on faces and objects on tables, the books people were reading, the games they were playing. He took pleasure in catching the expression of an old lady with a pixie face engrossed in a French novel. He lingered on a young man staring dreamily out of the window into a field of yellow flowers.

Most of the passengers were asleep and Sam stole their faces while they dreamt. Sleeping faces are a gift to the camera. There is in sleep an angel of distortion and a demon of beauty. In the far corner a man slept with his mouth wide open. Across, at a table of four, a child was asleep with its head tilted back in its mother's arms. A girl in jeans and a yellow blouse lay with her head on the shoulder of her sleeping boyfriend. Sleep had

34

given the girl charm, the boyfriend anxiety, the child abandon, and the grandfather who slept by the window an expression half grotesque, half benign.

While Sam filmed these faces, Lao was tempted to essay a character-reading of faces in sleep. Do criminals reveal their criminality while they doze? Do killers reveal a murderous aspect? What do our faces tell about us when we sleep, when we cannot hide the mind's construction in the face? What aspect of us comes through?

Sam had finished stealing faces in the carriage, and had passed on to the next. But Lao went on eviling, staring at faces, seeing cracks here, delighting in ugliness there. He thought of Da Vinci's grotesques, and revelled in the wicked humour of sleep.

CHAPTER 5

The train sped past a landscape with blue flowers, a countryside with an ochre church, farmlands with oxen and tractors. Lao was stuck in his eviling. The mood of evil-mindedness had settled in him like a gnome. He couldn't seem to shift it.

Staring at the red fabric of the seats and at the faces tinged with the redness, curious notions jumped into his mind. If travel is an escape, he thought, might we not be carrying with us the very things we are trying to escape?

At that moment the train plunged into a tunnel, there was a momentary blackout and Lao caught a glimpse of a figure at the window, attired like a dark magician. Again Malasso's name slid into his mind. With a bow the figure pointed at something behind Lao and then vanished.

When Lao looked round he saw, in a flash, a horrible spectacle. He saw imps of regret, goblins of worry, red-eyed monsters of nasty thoughts, giants of deeds done, hybrid creatures of fear, ghommids of envy, bats of guilt, cloven-hoofed figures of lust, beings of terrible aspect. He realised they were the problems, fears, nightmares, worries, and guilt that people carried around with them. It seemed everyone's troubles had accompanied them and crowded the compartment.

Lao saw them all in his eviling. He had seen them at the beginning of the journey, but had forgotten them. He noticed that not all the monsters had continued on the journey. Some might have dissolved on the way. Others might be lingering behind at immigration, faithful servants awaiting their master's return. But most of the creatures were still on the train.

Our past obscures our future, Lao thought, grimly. We travel forwards, but live backwards. Travelling is no escape; only the panorama changes. We are stuck in ourselves. There is no escape, but maybe there can be a change of direction. Maybe true travel is not the transportation of the body, but a change of perception, renewing the mind.

CHAPTER 6

Lao dozed off in the midst of these thoughts and when he woke he saw that Mistletoe was back. Her drawing book had been put aside and she was asleep with an innocent smile on her face. Lao imagined that she must have been a happy child before life brought her some unhappiness. He could see that travel brought back a measure of her happy childhood.

Maybe, Lao mused, staying in one place makes our monsters loom too large. Travelling gives them something to do. When we travel we take our troubles for a walk.

Maybe our monsters want their own Arcadia, somewhere they can be at peace, Lao thought, laughing to himself.

Then Mistletoe woke up, scanned the world beyond the window, and said:

'We're near Switzerland.'

'That figures,' Lao said.

'Why do you say that?'

He shrugged. 'Just when I'm beginning to understand something, we always arrive.'

'I know,' Mistletoe said. 'Journeys are perverse.

We arrive at our destination before we arrive at our revelation.'

'Did you just make that up?'

'I don't know. It just slipped into my mind.'

'Maybe it's the spirit of the journey,' Lao said.

CHAPTER 7

They did not notice how the journey was altering them. They did not notice how each place they had arrived at, stayed in, and passed through, was subtly transforming them. When they got off the train, they also did not notice the purity of the air, or the late afternoon light, or the porcelain blue of the sky. They were too engaged with the hassle of disembarkation. Jim gathered the troops together and each person was not only responsible for their own suitcases, but also for carrying down the film equipment in its tough cases.

A sort of military mood came over them as they got their luggage off the train at Basel. They had twenty-two pieces altogether. The luggage seemed to have acquired new weight, to have grown in size. Grown also was the crew's capacity to bear it. It was as though their luggage had made them stronger.

Riley, with her fragile frame, carried the heavy camera cases as though she had become a slender female Hercules. Sam, with professional stoicism, helped his young assistant. Everyone pitched in

– Propr, the temperamental sound man; Jute, the dour manager; Husk, with her nervous beauty; Mistletoe, with her smile; and Lao, presenter and poet. All pitched in, silently.

And even as they struggled with the chaos of their baggage, they were being worked on by the theme of their journey.

CHAPTER 8

Is there a name for that peculiar feeling of getting off trains? The hermeticists say that things on earth are mortal counterparts of things in heaven. Plato's ideal forms express the same idea. The person on a train does not move across a landscape: it is the vehicle that moves. But there is an illusion of movement. A train is a bridge between two realities, a space that enables people to take stock, to dream, to muse. It gives a sense of freedom. Maybe that is why people like train journeys.

At the end of a long train journey a phase is over. Gone is the fluidity of the place between. A new reality beckons.

To arrive means to become defined. To be, to do, to be done to. It may also mean having serious work to accomplish, with no time to adjust.

CHAPTER 9

Their battle with the luggage, conducted grimly, had a comic side. Their boxes and cases were heavy and resistant. They fell when they were lifted, they acquired odd angles that made them more than an armful, and they managed to achieve all kinds of collisions between those carrying them. The luggage took on a life of its own, as though impregnated with the spirit of perversity. It became abstract and severe. Those rectangular shapes, those faceless lumps that people lug around with them, made the travellers seem like sinners with their sins in Hades.

Those inanimate objects, crammed tight and bolted, that carry useless necessities, mean everything to travellers and nothing. To lose the luggage would be traumatic but not fatal; and yet they drag their luggage behind them like crimes, like secrets.

CHAPTER 10

Lao paused in his shifting and carrying and again a presence passed across his eyes. He saw the monsters had also come off the train. He realised that the monsters had not been left behind. They had merely grown more invisible on the journey, till it was as though they were not there.

Skulking behind the twenty-two pieces of luggage were the monsters they had brought with them. On the station platform they were getting acquainted with one another.

Lao was astonished to see his ghommids chatting with Jim's trolls, to see Jute's niebelungen gibbering with Riley's gnomes, Sam's harpies conversing with Mistletoe's sprite. They seemed to keep no secrets from one another. They talked and laughed about their owners as if the evils they knew about gave them much amusement.

CHAPTER 11

Lao saw all this, but didn't register it. He didn't really grasp it at the time.

'What are you looking at?' Jim said as Lao stood there staring at the stacks of luggage.

'Nothing,' Lao said, shaking his head. 'It's just that, for a moment, it seemed as if . . .'

'Are you seeing things?'

'I think so. I'm not sure.'

Jim slapped him on the back.

'Join the club,' he said, and went off to supervise the moving of the film equipment.

The luggage that had been hauled off the train had been piled high on a motorised trolley and driven off to the exit, where it was to be loaded on to their waiting coach.

Lao stood on the platform aware that a theme-note was being played in him, with its variations and inversions. As he watched the others head for the exit, after all their exertion, it seemed to him that there were two kinds of experience in life: the experience of the moment as it is lived and the experience of it afterwards when the whole is sensed. Micro-experience, and macro-experience.

He watched the twenty-two pieces of luggage being driven away. There are twenty-two letters in the Jewish alphabet, twenty-two cards in the major arcana of Tarot, and twenty-two paths on the tree of life. He only discovered this synchronicity much later.

Then he would pay attention to the small print in the text of life.

CHAPTER 12

While waiting for the luggage to be loaded on to the bus, Lao went wandering in the station. He came upon a large object on a plinth. All wheels and pulleys, it was like a whirring mechanical insect and it made screeching factory noises. He felt he was seeing something familiar in an unfamiliar guise. The machine disturbed him and he had to find out what it was.

Something about his encounter with the mechanical sculpture suggested the strangely pleasant feeling of being in the midst of a language he did not understand. And because he understood nothing, everything took on the quality of an encryption. Objects appeared in a new light.

Lao wandered down passageways, reading signs on doors and walls. He had the curious sensation of seeing objects separated from the names by which he knew them. They became unfixed: they became ideas again.

As he wandered past shops and kiosks, the people hurrying past did not seem to notice him, and he too began to feel unfixed, separated from his function, his name. At first the feeling was disquieting; he felt himself dissolve into anonymity. But then the sensation of fluidity grew on him, and he felt that he could become anyone, or no one.

Brushing past crowds of strangers in suits and dresses, with handbags, or briefcases, hurrying from work, or to meetings, or just commuting – walking among them – he felt momentarily free of the law he had invoked and set in motion: the law that says you are what you think you are. He also felt free of the other, more pernicious, law: the one that says you are what the world thinks you are.

For a moment Lao felt free of the prison of the constructed self, free also from the tyranny of attachment to things.

He wandered through the station gazing at faces, at designs on the walls, noting the great height of the ceiling, the quality of the light, the kind of clothes people wore, the obscure headlines in newspapers.

Seeing familiar things in a new light filled him with unexpected vitality. He felt like a convalescent: he felt he could begin to live again. He had a curious sense of remission. More than that, he felt stealing into him something of the enchantment of the first day in the garden. He had wandered into a happy state of mind.

I would like to master the art of living, he thought, and suddenly he heard demonic laughter somewhere behind him. He turned round but could not identify the source of the laughter. Again the name Malasso slipped into his mind.

Look at how difficult it is to master the art of writing, painting, composition; why should the art of living be any easier, he asked himself?

He went on walking about the station, looking at sweets and books in the well-lit shops, struck by the clean large windows.

The first freedom is freedom of mind, he thought; maybe, even, freedom from mind.

He didn't know it at the time but there, in the train station, of all places, he had experienced a bit of Eden.

BOOK III

A MOMENT WITH THE DEVIL

CHAPTER 1

Then he lost it. He lost the moment. He may have lost it because he looked back.

He had found himself in the central hall of the station, with its crowds and its giant screens on which flickered train destinations, times of departure, platform numbers. He was fascinated by the sight of travellers gazing intently up at the screens, trying to find their trains. As he watched he remembered a similar moment some days before in the Gare de l'Est, as they were leaving Paris.

The intensity with which the travellers now stared at the consoles reminded him of *Et in Arcadia ego*, the painting by Poussin that had transfixed the crew at the Louvre. In that enigmatic painting four shepherds in Arcadia have come upon a tomb which bears the famous inscription that provides the painting's title. The shepherds are staring at the inscription in a manner similar to the commuters in the train station. The similarity, a little tenuous perhaps, surprised Lao.

He found himself thinking about Poussin's painting in a new way. Were the shepherds happy before they came upon the tomb? Were they losing their happiness as they read the strange inscription? Are we all like the shepherds in the painting, trying to decipher the enigma?

Lao pursued the parallels between the painting and the travellers staring at the console. It seemed to him that, like the shepherds, we wander through the dream-like landscape of life, through days that pass so inevitably until one day we come upon the unavoidable fact of death. Then, like the shepherds, we try to read the mysterious inscription that is written on all mortal things.

It is an inscription written on all departure boards. It is the name of all destinations, but not our destiny. It is written on all faces, the great and the small. It is whispered in our triumphs and our failures.

Aren't we all trying to read the inscription on the tomb, Lao thought? Aren't we all shepherds trying to make sense of the small print in the text of life?

CHAPTER 2

Lao engaged in a little thought experiment. He began to think of the shepherds in the painting. He saw them as real living people – people that he knew. He imagined them tending their flock and larking about. He imagined a perfect summer's day in the mountains of Arcadia. Then he imagined the shepherds coming upon this tomb with its curious inscription.

How long does it take them to read the words? Did they read Latin? Each letter is an unfolding mystery.

The words are read. *Et in Arcadia ego. I too have lived in Arcadia.* They look at one another. They have read the words, but what do they mean? They read the words again. The real reading begins when the first reading is over. It begins with their bewilderment.

Meanwhile what has happened to the four shepherds? They are not the people that they were. The inscription has thrown them back on themselves. They are troubled because they do not understand.

Suddenly a question mark quivers over all things.

The beautiful landscape is no longer what it seems. The perfect summer's day now hints at something sinister.

Reading was born, Lao thought, in that moment of exile from a previous state of grace.

CHAPTER 3

Lao realised, with a small shock, that the shepherds in the painting are engaged in an eternal act of reading. All they will ever do is read that inscription and try to make sense of it. They are perpetual readers. And in their endless deciphering something awakes in them.

It occurred to Lao that we too are intrigued by the words because we recognise them. We utter the inscription at the beginning and at the end. It was in our birth cry. It will be in our deaths, as the significance of our tombs. We write those words – *I too have lived in Arcadia* – as a memento to ourselves, to remind us who we are, where we have been, where we are now, and where we are going.

In Basel station Lao lost the golden moment when he made the link between people gazing at the departure boards and the shepherds in Arcadia reading words on a tomb.

CHAPTER 4

Malasso continued to haunt all of them. The haunting took forms so subtle that, at first, no one noticed.

After the luggage had been transported to the coach, and Sam had taken continuity shots of Lao's arrival at the station, they were driven to their hotel in the town of B— through the falling darkness.

Their driver was a tall eager fresh-faced young man called Bruno. He was the second Bruno of their journey, the first being their driver in France. Lao thought of this new driver as Bruno the Second.

In the bus everyone seemed sombre and tired. The journey had taken its toll. Only Bruno was lively. With youthful enthusiasm he kept asking them questions. From his driver's seat he asked where they were going, whether it was a feature film they were making, and whether it would be shown in cinemas in Switzerland. He asked what Arcadia meant, and whether they would film him and make him famous. He was in high spirits, and practising his English. He got monosyllabic replies.

They drove from Basel northwest on Münsterplatz, and went from Rittergasse to Wettsteinbrücke. Lao saw the names as they drove. Too tired to gaze at the small print of Swiss life, he gazed at the large print instead. The coach turned into Grenzacherstrasse and they were soon on a toll road. He saw signs for Luzern, Gotthard, and Rothrist. The place names mesmerised him. In his exhaustion he was looking forward to two days of rest. He should have been cautious about days of rest. That's when hidden things strike, when the small print bites.

They drove for hours. They drove through neat towns with rectilinear houses. They drove past white disembodied forms in the air, past unseen mountains.

Husk and Riley sat together, getting on famously. Every now and then they talked in loud whispers punctuated with prolonged giggling. Husk was prim, Riley something of a pixie, but the journey revealed the things they had in common. Jute sat alone, grim as ever, as if she hadn't smiled for decades. Propr too sat alone, near the front of the coach. His moustache concealed his mood. He was always melancholic when he had nothing to do.

Sam, the cameraman, also sat towards the front, on a seat all by himself. He played with his ponytail and stared out of the window. He was in a thoughtful mood. It had been a good day filming and he had caught many wonderful shots of the mountains and the passengers in different states of contemplation, sleep, or empty-mindedness. He had also taken a few more difficult shots which pleased him. It was the difficult ones that really made a day of filming worthwhile for him. But work was over now for the day, and as the coach drove past charming towns with well-lit houses where perfectly ordered middle-class lives were being lived, a thoughtful look came over him. His mind was empty and he was not thinking of anything in particular. As he looked at the suburban houses he entertained a passing longing for a domestic Arcadia. As a cameraman he was always away on one shoot or another and it wouldn't be unusual to have such a yearning without even being aware of it. He had a touching look on his face. He may have become aware of that yearning for, a moment later, he switched on his reading light and turned his attention to Camus' *Selected Essays*. Sam thought of himself as an existentialist.

Jim, the director, sat towards the back of the coach. He was wide awake, making lists and calculations in his notebook. He wasn't paying much attention to the world outside the coach, to the well-made houses and the symmetrically planted trees. Jolted every now and again by the swerving of the bus, he would look up from his work, stare blankly ahead, and plunge back into his lists and diagrams, anecdotes and calculations.

Lao, sitting nearby, found his eyes drawn by the words on a page of Jim's open notebook. The reading light shone on the page and the words were unavoidable. They made Lao shudder, as if he had seen inside the director's mind. In horror and amazement he saw, written vertically in capital letters down the page: KILL MALASSO. The page was festooned with violent images, a knife, a gun, skull and crossbones, a swastika, a grinning face without eyes. Then, over the course of the journey in the dark, Lao saw Jim compose from each letter of the words an acrostic poem:

> Kings do not dream at night
> In lonely castles by the sea.
> Love does not respond to might;
> Love, if true, must be free.
> Murder could end this deal.
> Allow blood to stream the stars.
> Lend the film the truth of the unreal
> And to the viewer distracted hours.
> Sow havoc among Arcadians
> Show them death in flowers
> Or treat them like barbarians.

Jim spent most of the coach ride writing this poem. And when he had finished he switched off his reading light, and gave a little laugh in the dark.

CHAPTER 5

For the first time on their journey, it occurred to Lao that Jim was cracked, that life had driven him over the edge.

The laughter, more than a little fiendish, and very uncharacteristic, went on ringing in Lao's head. No one else seemed to have heard it. But Mistletoe, who had been asleep, woke up, and looked about her like a startled bird. Then she stared out of the window into the ink-coloured sky.

Lao began wondering why Jim's disturbed mental state had not become clear earlier. As he ran his mind over the whole journey he found memories that so mixed the sane with the ambivalent that nothing stood out.

In the darkness, Jim was stabbing at his notebook with his pen, and tittering to himself.

The mood of the coach was heavy with silence and sleep. Even Sam who had been reading was asleep. He had been re-reading Camus' introduction to his essays and had come upon the following lines: *The place where I prefer to live and work (and something more rare, where I would not mind dying) is a hotel bedroom. I have never felt capable of indulging*

62

in what they call home life (which is so often the opposite of an inner life); bourgeois happiness bores and terrifies me. The words had set up a conflict in Sam, had disturbed him, and he had paused to stare out into the dark countryside. Unable to settle his thoughts he had flicked through the book till he came to an essay called 'The Desert'. It was an essay about Florence. He would read a few lines and drift off into reverie. *Living, of course, is slightly the opposite of expressing.* This made him think. *What counts is not poetry. What counts is truth.* This made him question his art. *But sadness in this country is never anything but a commentary on beauty. And as the train travelled on through the evening I felt a tension in me slowly giving way.* This made Sam marvel at its appositeness. *We must learn how to lend ourselves to dreams when dreams lend themselves to us.* This made him drift off. Soon Camus' essays lay on his lap, pages open, existentialism read by the night.

Lao listened to the world rush by as the coach hurtled down the winding roads. Bruno had a fixed expression in his eyes. He drove as if he were in a movie.

CHAPTER 6

Lao reconsidered Jim's case.

It has been said that when someone sets out to change their life in some way the demons in the psyche rise up and all one's habits protest. The old dispensation rises in revolt and it can feel as if one were going mad. Psychologists say that this is not surprising. After all one is trying to change the existing order, to dethrone the old king. Forces in the psyche will not let this happen without a punishing fight. That fight can feel like insanity.

It had often occurred to Lao that something terrifying attends the heels of change. He had heard that those who are trying to overcome addiction often report shooting pains in the head, hallucinations, night-sweats, nightmares, panic attacks, sudden sweeps of hot emotions, rages, mood-swings, rampant desires – civil war in the soul.

They are, more or less, hints from the *ancien régime* that the old life is best. They are powerful persuasions against change.

That is the power of habit, Lao thought. It has

64

the force of demons. Alarmed by the convulsions tricked up by the old guard, most people abandon their attempts at change. It can seem more trouble than it is worth. Who can say that change will be better? It might be worse. It might be boring. The old dispensation, thought Lao, always appears indispensable.

The worse the revolts, the closer to victory. The demons have the best weapons: they have one's past. The angels have only one's possible future. The past is more real than the future. But to make that crossing to a possible future, a death must take place. The old self must die. Lao remembered an African saying: *The seed must die before it can grow*. He had heard that people who are on the verge of major changes in their lives often dream they are drowning, or that they are in car crashes in which they die. The curious thing about those dreams, Lao often remarked, is that the dreamers who witness their own deaths do not die.

CHAPTER 7

They say that to find order one must go through chaos, to attain success one must pass through the polished gates of failure. Lao wondered whether to arrive at Arcadia one must venture through madness.

In Virgil's *Eclogues*, one of the primary texts that shaped the idea of Arcadia, there is a sinister intuition. Something in the landscape of Arcadia creates inner disorder. Some of the dwellers in Arcadia are haunted by madness and extreme passions. This had always bothered Lao. He was never sure why madness lurked among Virgil's shepherds. Lao often thought that maybe Virgil had intuited the power of the god Pan, or maybe that lonely shepherds in mountains are prey to obsessions.

Was the quest for Arcadia driving Jim mad? When a man as harmless as Jim takes to writing words of murderous intent it is reasonable to consider his sanity.

Why does he want to kill Malasso anyway, Lao wondered? None of the film crew had ever seen

Malasso. No one knew what he looked like. No one knew whether he even existed. Wanting to kill him therefore was itself a sign of disturbed thinking.

CHAPTER 8

Lao listened to Jim breathing deeply in his sleep. Then, to Lao's surprise, Jim dug an elbow into his ribs. Lao turned to look at him but could only make out the snarled outline of his face in the dark.

'I've just had this dream, in which I had a long chat with the Devil,' Jim said.

'Really?' Lao replied.

'He told me what to do.'

'To do about what?'

'The Devil only tells you what to do one step at a time.'

'Why?'

Lao could feel rather than see Jim shrug. The outline of his face showed caverns and shadows.

'Our destiny is not our destination,' Jim said, with an odd, knowing laugh.

'But what did he tell you to do?'

'What do you mean?'

'You said the Devil told you what to do.'

'Yes.'

'About what?'

There was a long pause. The coach sliced

smoothly through the night. Its purring engine was now muffled and distant. The coach tore down winding roads. Inside it was still and dark. Lao thought Jim had fallen asleep again. Then came the voice, new, clear, unreal.

'To square the circle, control the factors, master the chaos, fulfil my wishes.'

He paused and said, as if thinking aloud:

'Suddenly, one day, I will emerge as one of the great masters of my art, and everyone will be astounded.'

The unreality of what Jim said lingered in the air a moment. He made a face in the dark, re-arranging its lines into something ironic.

'Jim?'

'Yes.'

'Have you been drinking?'

'Have I been thinking?'

'No. Drinking. Have you been drinking?'

'No, I haven't been drinking. I am as sober as a newscaster.'

The idea of a drunken newscaster made Lao smile.

'Have you been reading Goethe's *Faust*?'

'You mean as research for our visit to the Goetheanum?'

'No, I mean have you been reading too much Faust?'

'No more than necessary. Why?'

'It's because of all this Devil stuff and being told what to do by him in a dream.'

Jim laughed again. Even his laughter was unreal. Can a man change so quickly, Lao wondered? Maybe it's just that he is breathing better. His laughter sounded at once very sane and a little mad.

After a short pause, during which the register of his voice shifted, and in a tone that was clear and firm, Jim said:

'Many years ago, when I craved success more than anything else in the world, I offered to sell my soul to the Devil.'

'Really?'

'Yes.'

There was a long silence.

'But he wouldn't have me.'

'Why not?'

'He said my soul wasn't good enough.'

Lao stared at him with faint incredulity.

'He said my soul wasn't interesting enough. It was too mild. It didn't have enough potential for good or for evil.'

Jim unburdened himself of a mildly unhinged chuckle.

'Apparently I have a middling soul. The soul of an English sheep.'

He paused. His voice turned more serious.

'Apparently I have an ordinary will. The sort of chap who would vote with the crowd. The kind who keeps his head below the parapet. Would always choose the safe option. Not much use to God or Satan. Middle of the road. Always muddling through. You know the type. The country is populated with us. Maybe, even, the world.'

He paused again, and his features in the dark rearranged themselves into what Lao realised was a smile. A light from a passing car revealed Jim's eyes. Heaven help us, Lao thought, sitting up straight. It seemed to him that Jim was possessed, and that a hint of evil had brought out his true personality.

Lao turned to face him; a question he had not prepared sprang from his lips.

'Jim, how does one sell one's soul to the Devil? I mean how does one actually do it?'

Jim flashed Lao a look so piercing and unexpected that he felt the back of his neck go cold.

'Why?' asked Jim with cool irony. 'Is your soul up for sale?'

Lao tried to stay calm. He struggled for the right response.

'I just wondered how it works,' he said.

Jim invested Lao with a long candid scrutiny. Lao was not sure if it constituted an evaluation of his soul, and whether, in Jim's estimation, the Devil might be interested in its purchase. Jim's silence was inconclusive. When he eventually spoke it was with quiet authority.

CHAPTER 9

'Nearly driven insane by the astonishing success of some of my mediocre colleagues,' Jim said, 'I fell on my knees one night and summoned the Devil. I did this, following an ancient prescribed ritual that I found in an antiquarian bookshop, for seven consecutive nights. And then, after my blood was involved, he appeared.'

'He appeared?' Lao asked incredulously.

'He appeared, in my room, in person, in all his satanic majesty. He was not at all what I expected.'

'What did you expect?'

'He was not ugly, he had no horns, he had no hoofs, and no fires burned around him. His aura was not horrible.'

'What was he like?' Lao asked in the voice of a child.

'He had a very sweet smell,' said Jim, without drama. 'He was simply dazzling. I realised at once that he had indeed been one of the brightest angels in heaven. His charm and beauty were seductive beyond belief. He was the image of the most successful, the most famous, and the most youthful person you can imagine. You sensed, in his presence, that he knew everything. And there he was, in person, in my house, in Kent.'

Jim paused. He appeared to be musing. Occasionally a street lamp would light up his face. After a moment he continued in the same tone as before.

'His presence brightened the house and glamorised everything in his vicinity. The Devil, as I saw him, was beautiful, delightful, thoughtful, reasonable, and kind. He understood everything. His conversation was exquisite. I had never known before that conversation could be one of the ecstasies of life.'

He paused again, like one whose every memory was a rare pearl which had to be examined in a magical light. Then he shook his head, and turned on Lao an intense pair of eyes that burned with cherished reminiscence.

'He was the very incarnation of seduction,' said Jim quietly. 'I would have done anything for him.'

A longer pause followed, and a drop in his tone, as his voice became more contemplative.

'When someone is better than you expect them to be, you are already halfway seduced. When someone is worse than you expect, you are halfway repelled. The Devil seduced me not by anything he did or said. He seduced me with his serenity.'

Jim gave an airy little laugh.

'Isn't that strange?'

Lao didn't know what to say. He was so

fascinated that he was wholly unaware of the motion of the coach through the dark countryside. Jim sighed.

'He didn't try to sell me atheism, humanism, existentialism, evil dogmas, satanic rituals, or any such thing. He didn't rail against God, religion, or purity. He didn't offer me the world. He didn't try to buy me. He didn't promise me the kingdoms of fame or success. In fact, to my chagrin, he wasn't interested. He was cool. He wasn't buying, and he wasn't selling.'

Jim stopped again, and then, in an odd rhythm, he said:

'I would have given him everything.'

Then what followed was something close to a sob. Then a long sigh, like a lingering regret.

'He had only appeared because I had so insistently summoned him. He was, it seemed, mildly curious about me. But his curiosity was such, I sensed, that he already knew the answer. He was very polite. I had the distinct feeling that he might be interested in me in the future, if I ever did anything extraordinary. He seemed to know I mightn't. I would dearly love to surprise him.'

The coach was slowing down, the purr of the engine became a growl, and then turned smoother. Lao was only dimly conscious of this. Jim's words had him enthralled, as though he too were under a seduction. Jim shifted his position in the seat, and was almost upright, his face lost in thought.

'He actually said very little. In fact, I'm not sure that he uttered a single word.'

Jim turned and touched Lao on the shoulder, as if to secure his utmost attention.

'I think he appeared to me mainly because he was interested to hear exactly how I would pose the question.'

Jim drew a deep breath and, very gently, said:

'It was the greatest moment of my life.'

'Jim!' cried Lao, unable to contain his astonishment.

Jim chuckled and tapped the poet on his forearm.

'You would never have guessed it to look at me, would you?'

Lao shook his head, quite dumbfounded. Then realising that Jim could not see the gesture, he said:

'No, Jim, I wouldn't have.'

Jim chuckled again.

'Failure often leads us to the most interesting places,' he said, with mischievous timing.

They had arrived at the hotel.

One of Lao's lasting regrets was that he didn't ask Jim how he had posed the great question. For Jim never opened himself to Lao in that way ever again.

CHAPTER 10

They staggered down from the coach and, working together as a group, they lugged the camera equipment and baggage into the hotel lobby.

It was a modest family hotel on the edge of Lake Lucerne. The owner was a pleasant middle-aged down-to-earth man called Hans. With his fine moustache, he could have played a medieval innkeeper in a European movie. He was charming to the weary film crew but treated Lao with a certain undefined suspicion.

They were checked in, allocated their rooms, and encouraged to inspect them. They were all delighted with their accommodation and Hans made sure they were comfortably settled, and arranged for the carrying of their luggage to their various rooms.

Lao felt left outside this ring of affection. He was convinced that Hans behaved differently towards him. He listened with an ironic smile to the crew members talking about how excellent the hotel was and how nice Hans had been to them. Lao did not feel that Hans had been so nice to him. He felt the others could not see this because Hans's attitude was visible to him alone.

As what is not seen is not believed, there were no witnesses to this double-handed treatment. Lao didn't make a fuss because he knew he would only come across as paranoid or oversensitive. And so he decided, as he always did, to bear the matter with dignity. He decided also to try to win Hans over with charm. But to be on the safe side he asked Mistletoe to deal with the hotel owner on their behalf. Mistletoe didn't mind.

They had been allocated rooms which Lao insisted on changing till he found one which was acceptable. He finally settled for a room on the first floor, a lovely double room with a fine balcony and a perfect view of the lake and the Rigi mountain. And it was, auspiciously, room seven.

After Lao and Mistletoe had settled in, they had their showers, changed into fresh clothes, and went out on to the balcony.

The mountain was not visible. It was simply a great looming darkness, festooned with twinkling lights, like stars clustered in a nebula. Sprinkled across the invisible mountain were constellations of small towns.

The shimmering waters of the lake made a

magical contrast to the dark mass of the mountain. Lao contemplated the nature of water, its responsiveness, the way it transforms its environment. Mistletoe, seated a short distance away from him, surrendered herself to a sense of wonder and timelessness. The lake cast a spell over the world.

In their own rooms, the other members of the crew were experiencing the same wonder as they gazed out across the lake.

Nature had begun to work on them, loosening the holds of their demons, making them feel lighter. For some this brought moments of joy, to others terror. To some their demons are an intrinsic part of what they are; to lose their demons would be to lose their identity.

The silence of the mountains makes inward troubles apparent. Many prefer motion to stillness.

Lao and Mistletoe preferred stillness. As they sat on their balcony they realised they had forgotten what it was like to stare in uncomplicated wonder, at a lake in the dark, at lights on a mountainside, at a calm sky. Distant bells sounded on the breeze. There was laughter down below. They felt as if they had been transported from their bodies by a god and delivered to a realm of pure delight. Then they heard music across the lake, and held their breath.

Arcadia is a dream, and dreams infect reality with their truth.

Mistletoe would remember that moment as one of the purest of her life. Lao would forever associate it with a certain half-lit landscape in paradise.

CHAPTER 11

When they went down to dinner they found that all was not well. Everyone looked a little distressed, seated gloomily round a long table. Jim's thinning hair was unkempt, his eyes distracted. Propr's moustache was all awry, as if he had twisted it into the visual image of his mood. Jute sat in monumental impassivity. Riley seemed to have shrunk below the rim of the table. Sam didn't know where to hide his eyes. Husk sat there, saying nothing, but managed to spread a toxic atmosphere.

Lao looked at Jim enquiringly.

'Bad news from home,' he said, in a whisper.

Lao and Mistletoe found seats for themselves. A waitress came to take their orders but the atmosphere was so forbidding that she stood there staring. No one spoke to her, so she left.

Husk was eviling. Her eyes were narrowed in pain and bitterness. She kept to herself the bad news that she had received. But she sat there and poured out an evil mood.

Her eyes were troubling. No one could quite look at her. Eviling eyes are as bad as evil deeds.

Such a person seems capable of worse things than they really are. No one forgets a witnessed eviling. Suspicion about one seen doing it can last a lifetime. But everyone dwells under the inexplicable cloud of a foul mood at some time or another. The crew round the table concentrated too much on Husk. Her mood fed on their attention.

The cutlery shone on the tables in the dining room, and the glasses glittered in the light of the chandeliers. Couples were having quiet dinners in distant corners. A Schubert Quintet swam through the atmosphere.

Round their table they all took Husk's eviling personally. Maybe it was because in their rooms, looking out at the lake, feeling the breeze on their faces, they had glimpsed a moment of beauty. There is something poisonous about eviling in the midst of happiness.

CHAPTER 12

The human spirit knows how to protect itself from these things, Lao was thinking, when Mistletoe rose like a dryad from her chair. She went round to Husk, embraced her like a twin sister, and gave her a gift-wrapped present.

'Happy birthday,' she said.

Husk blushed.

'I didn't think anyone knew,' she said, tears sparkling in her eyes.

All at once they crowded round Husk, hugging and consoling her, bringing out gifts and cards they had carried around in secret. They lavished on her much affection and soon pleasure replaced the bitterness on her face.

Joy flowed with her tears. Though they didn't know what they were consoling her for, nor what privation she was enduring, they managed to revive her spirits.

When they had all gone back to their seats, Propr tapped a knife against a glass and cried:

'Speech, Husk, speech!'

'And make it brief,' Jim teased, 'we've got a film to finish.'

Husk smiled; everyone laughed. Her smile was infectious. It lifted the general mood. She seemed inspired.

'About birthdays there is not much to say. One was born on a certain day, so so many years ago . . .'

'Reveal! Reveal!' cried Lao.

Husk smiled indulgently, and continued.

'And one moves closer to one's death. Every birthday is a dying . . .'

'You are not allowed to be gloomy today,' said Riley, touching her on the shoulder.

Husk gave an uncertain smile.

'A dying and a being born. We get worse, we get better, we try to sing the song. It is not an especially happy birthday for me, but it is special because of you all. You've all been so generous. Who shall I thank first? Lao, how did you know I love Gregorian chants? You've got good spies. Mistletoe, you have a gift for bringing out the best in situations. Thank you for tonight. Jute, without you this journey wouldn't have got this far . . .'

'And may not get further, at this rate,' Jim said, initiating a pattern of subsequent high-spirited interruptions.

'Riley, thanks for the scarf and for your quirkiness. Where did Sam find such a wonderful and elusive assistant?'

'In the Black Forest, pecking away at life,' said Jim.

'And you, Sam. Are the dark glasses meant to stop me seeing what you are up to . . .?'

'Up to no good, if I can help it,' Sam rejoined.

'Propr, salt of the earth . . .' Husk continued.

'Sound of the earth,' said Lao.

'Sound of the wind,' said Jim.

'Boys, boys!' said Husk.

'Let her finish her assassinations,' said Propr.

'Surely you mean insinuations,' said Jim.

'I meant assassinations,' said Propr, with solemn humour.

'Propr,' said Husk, 'we all love your sense of right proportion . . .'

'I like that! Right propr-ortion! Ha, ha, ha . . .' laughed Jim.

'And you, Jim . . .'

'Jim, here comes the knife!' said Lao.

'It'll be no worse than the wife . . .' said Jim.

'Oh, we are getting versy.'

'Jim, the last time I did a film shoot with you . . .'

'Everyone died except you two,' said Propr.

'It was so bad no one knew what to do,' added Sam.

Husk gave Sam a stern look.

'I was only joking. Surely you know that. Can't one joke any more?'

'The last time only five minutes of a three week shoot got aired,' Husk finished.

'I know, I know,' said Jim bitterly. 'I could have killed them.'

The mood changed a little. Jim stood up and sat down again. While they had been talking, bottles of Pinot Noir and Sauvignon, ordered by Jim, had been opened at the table. Jim was the only one who had been drinking.

'You are the best,' Husk said, reassuringly, trying to keep the good spirits that had found a home round the table. 'But this idea of a journey to Arcadia, where did you get it? I still can't get my head round it.'

'It was his idea,' Jim said, pointing at Lao.

'Not me. It was his,' said Lao, pointing at Sam.

'Not me, his,' Sam gestured at Propr.

'It came from the Black Forest,' growled Propr.

'I don't even know what the word means,' said Riley, in her elfin voice. 'It must have come from her,' pointing at Jute.

'Not me, Guv. It was her.'

She looked at Mistletoe. But Mistletoe was drawing. She was attempting quick portraits of individuals in the group. Picking up the circulating thread, she broke off her concentration, and said:

'It was Malasso's idea.'

There was a long pause. They could hear the wind outside.

'Malasso who must be obeyed,' Propr said, in a stage whisper.

'Why don't we stop bringing up that name. It gives me the creeps,' cried Jute.

Jim looked at the empty spaces around them. They were the only ones left in the dining room.

'He may be with us now even as we speak,' said Jim.

'Don't mess about. If he appeared here, right now, and announced himself, you would all faint,' said Jute.

'I am more practical,' said Propr. 'I would run.'

Mistletoe looked up from her drawing. She was sketching Riley now, and finding her as elusive as ever.

'Husk, I'm sorry I brought up that name,' she said. 'You hadn't finished your speech.'

'Yes, speech! Speech!'

'Shut up everyone, and let's hear the birthday girl,' said Jim.

Silence followed. The waitress came to take orders but was asked by Jim to come back in five minutes.

'I didn't get a chance to say what my Arcadia might be,' said Husk.

This provoked a chorus of voices.

'Yes, you did.'

'No, she didn't.'

'I didn't.'

'I want to change mine.'

'You can't change it.'

'Let Husk speak!'

The voices fell silent.

'My private Arcadia,' said Husk, 'would be finding a perfect moment and living in it forever.'

'That was Faust's deal with Mephistopheles,' said Lao.

'What?'

'That if he experienced the perfect . . .'

'Don't say any more. I want to change my Arcadia.'

'You only get one more wish, so let's hear it,' said Jim.

Husk thought for a moment. Jim filled everyone's glass with wine. Then Husk, in a bright clear voice, said:

'I would like to make every moment special when I'm living it and beautiful when I remember it. I have grown too serious as I've got older. I seem to make my own misery. I can't seem to help it. When I was a girl it felt like I was in paradise all the time . . .'

'You must have been a naughty girl,' said Jim.

'And I was always happy. I had the knack. I was happy whenever I wanted to be. It was as easy as stepping through a door. Then one day I lost it. I lost the knack. Something happened and I still don't know what it was. I became grim and got worse as the years passed. It's only now that I remember how happy I used to be. Only now do I remember that I had this ability. It was the only real talent I ever had, and I lost it before I got started.'

'And it's been a chequered journey ever since,' Jim said.

The silence that followed did two things. It gave everyone time to drink in Husk's words. And it made them aware that Jim was changing before their eyes.

CHAPTER 13

The waitress had come round a third time and finally taken their orders. They had all been drinking steadily. The freshness of the air and their increasing relaxation loosened their tongues and they passed from subject to subject, sometimes arguing, often talking at cross-purposes. Lao may have been thinking about the conversation with Jim on the coach; or he may simply have been responding to the tone of Jim's voice as he talked about the progress of the film so far; but everyone was a little taken aback when Lao said:

'The trouble with you, Jim, is that you use too much will.'

'And you,' replied Jim, entering the spirit of the joust, 'believe too little in the will.'

'For me the will is the engine.'

'What's wrong with that?'

'The driver, not the engine, should be in charge of the car.'

'The car is only as good as the engine.'

'But the engine shouldn't be in the driving seat. The car is only as good as the driver.'

'So what are you saying?'

'You believe too much in the will.'

'You're just lazy.'

'I'm not lazy. It's just that there are forces other than the will for accomplishing great things.'

'I don't agree. Will is the thing. What have you got against the will?'

'Nothing. It's a matter of the right thing in the right place. There's no doubt that the will gets things done; but it can just as well get the wrong thing done, in the wrong way, for the wrong reasons, at any cost. My point is that will is blind. It is like a machine. You can point it in any direction and it will go to the ends of the earth. Getting things done – any old thing – is not in itself desirable. Getting great things done – beautiful things – that is an ideal.'

'Give me an example.'

Lao paused, drank some of his red wine, then said:

'Let's say you have the idea to start a business. You think about it, shape the idea in your mind, make plans, and then you put the plans into action. You do something about it. Raising the money, finding an office, hiring staff, selling your product – all require will, constant will, but will only in the service of a clear practical vision. Otherwise the will might be in the service of a bad idea, or a good idea at the wrong time, and the result will not be success, but failure and bankruptcy. Will is an important partner, but a junior partner. With you it's the boss.'

'I disagree with you completely,' said Jim, turning his reddening face on Lao and then looking challengingly round the table.

Struck by the tone of Jim's voice, Mistletoe stopped her drawing and stared at him. She noticed how he had changed. She began a new portrait of him, the emerging lines following what the change suggested. The others were also struck by the bold new tone of his voice and leaned forward and listened to him anxiously. Only Lao remained calm.

Jim said:

'The will built nations, empires, civilisations. Every human achievement is founded on will. It is the quality that distinguishes human beings from animals . . .'

'No, it isn't,' said Lao. 'Mules and dogs, and horses in a race, have will . . .'

Jim rushed on in a kind of frenzy.

'Will is the basis of discipline, and without discipline nothing of any note is done. Our heroes are people of will: Napoleon and his forced marches that collapsed time, Alexander the Great and his astonishing feats of endurance, Picasso and his phenomenal energy, Churchill and his indomitable spirit . . .'

'All of them men,' said Jute.

'Wherever you see will at work the true steel in mankind is at the helm,' Jim went on. He paused and gathered in all the faces in a sweeping glance.

'Will distinguishes those who can from those

who can't. It is the single factor by which a man or woman', and here he gave Jute a pointed look, 'can rise to fame in their field of endeavour. All those who have climbed high cite the will as their climbing rope.'

'I wonder if that's true . . .' ventured Propr.

'Of course it is,' said Jim, with an expansive gesture of his hand. 'Desire alone never got anything done. Wishing is for the indolent. All this talk of visualisation and meditation – well, I've tried it all, and it doesn't work.'

'You were half-hearted, that's why,' said Husk. 'You probably didn't believe it would work anyway.'

'Not correct. I visualised till my eyes fell out, but the job went to the best prepared and the keenest.'

'There is a quotation of Ignatius Loyola you might find useful,' Sam said. 'He suggests that we use the things of God as if earthly means do not exist, and use earthly means as if God does not exist. I'm not sure if I quoted that right.'

Jim stared at Sam as if he had made a contribution of charming irrelevance. Then he shook his head and went on as if he had not been interrupted.

'The will is the right hand of the master. Seven years of willing transformed Van Gogh from a dissatisfied banker . . .'

'To a suicide,' said Propr.

'To a great artist. Beethoven's will was legendary, triumphing over the abyss and deafness. Where there's a will there's a way, the saying goes; and it is true. The will is akin to the power of the Demiurge. It makes worlds. It is the force that turns dreams into realities. It hews on earth castles in the air. Take the will out of the human story and we'd still be in the caves, without fire.'

'Fire was not discovered by will,' said Sam, 'but by chance.'

'How do you know?' replied Jim, turning fiery eyes on Sam. 'It takes will to rub two sticks together to make a flame. Will in man is a force that can make even the heavens tremble.'

'The first thing that tyrants do to their people,' said Jute in a calm, plain voice, 'is try to break their will.'

'Absolutely,' said Jim, not quite seeing the point of the comment. 'Intelligence is useless without will. That is why people can see what needs to be done but, lacking will, they let evil flourish. They allow menacing weeds to ruin the garden that is their nation. Even reason itself requires will. The reasoning of Newton is different from that of Propr.'

'There is nothing wrong with my powers of reasoning.'

'No, but you are not Newton. He reasoned with a tempered will. To think beyond the common range, till thought borders on genius, requires reason multiplied by the power of will. But lazy thinking predominates in our world. It takes will to think clearly.'

'You are making will into a god,' said Propr. 'It's a kind of idolatry.'

'Maybe, maybe not. But you show me a civilising quality and I will show you how the will holds it up like the Doric columns of a Greek temple.'

'Okay, what about love?' offered Riley.

'Love? Love is sustained by the will when, as is inevitable, it passes the early magic stages.'

Riley looked around, and grinned.

'You may smile, but there is a lull in the progression of all natural things. But will can take over till the rhythm of progression reasserts itself.'

Riley looked puzzled.

'Thus a poem begins well and dries out; a novel starts with a blaze and dwindles into inconsequence; love begins in bliss and soon hits the banks of disenchantment. But only will sees a way. Only will keeps things on track till affection blooms again.'

'You can't will love!' cried Husk, indignantly.

'No, but with will a less glamorous, but more steady love – the love on which all lasting marriages are based – takes over.'

'Still, you can't will it,' said Husk, in a Galileo *sotto voce.*

CHAPTER 14

Throughout the exchanges Lao had been silent and kept his eyes on Jim. He wore his ironic smile. While Jim was speaking Lao found his mind wandering back to the conversation in the coach but he refused to come to any conclusions. He would just listen.

Jim helped himself to wine and drank half the glass. There were murmurs round the table about the time their food was taking. Jim took a deep breath, tousled what was left of his hair, and returned to the charge.

'I should elaborate a bit more. The novel never gets written without will. It remains a beautiful idea to be bandied about at dinner parties. A film never gets made with mantras and meditation. Hard graft, the march of a thousand miles, and the willingness to sacrifice almost everything is what gets a film to the big screen. The will is the most direct translation of the life-force into deed. When you hear it said by a great artist that *my life is in those works* or *I wrote it with my blood*, you know that an exchange, a kind of Faustian pact, has been effected. Life-force for life work. The will is life-force.'

Lao smiled. His intuition had been right. Jim looked at him expectantly, but Lao stayed silent, and Jim continued.

'When the true life's work is done a man is fit for nothing but tending his garden and awaiting the flower of his death.'

'We're getting morbid tonight,' said Propr.

'Not really,' replied Jim, 'I'm just trying to show why the failures of those who have made great efforts move us so much.'

'Yes, they tried, made great efforts, but death defeated them,' said Sam. 'There is heroism in that too.'

Mistletoe had been following the general tenor of the conversation with her left ear, as it were, while she was drawing Jim. Without a pause, quietly, she said:

'The gods would rather we use our life than squander it.'

Everyone stared at her, unsure whether she was speaking to them, but Jim took it as a sign of concurrence and was encouraged to go on.

'As I was saying, those who perish in the struggle to turn their dreams into reality are more admirable than those who live and die without giving a sign that they were ever alive. One of the greatest legacies we can leave future generations is the knowledge that we fought the beautiful fight, played the game, bore arms. And if we are defeated by the bastards, crushed by mediocrity and the cliques that rule the world, then our defeat will spur on future generations. Behind most great men and women are defeated ancestors.'

Jim stared thoughtfully ahead, a lost look on his face. For a moment he seemed to have lost his point. He sipped some wine and began to speak again, as if thinking aloud.

'It's the will that pulls us up. Dante composed *The Divine Comedy* with a magnificent will that transcended calumny and exile. A baby wakens into life with a cry, its first breath is an act of will.'

'Not an act of will,' interrupted Sam. 'But of necessity . . .'

'Necessity is will,' said Jim, his voice rising. 'And will is at the beginning. Goethe wrote that in the beginning was the deed. And I add that the deed was willed.'

'I'd say inspired,' said Husk.

'Or dreamt into being,' said Mistletoe, from the depths of her drawing.

A ripple of silence followed. Outside, the wind was blowing. They were sitting round a table in an empty restaurant in Switzerland and it seemed to them dreamlike. A shiver passed through them, communicated from person to person.

'Thy will be done on earth as it is in heaven,' said Jim.

Husk crossed herself and Sam looked at her curiously as if seeing her for the first time.

'Notice,' said Jim, 'how much is made of God's will in the Lord's Prayer. It's just as true with the human will. Here, on earth, our will does the doing.'

'Is that even grammatical?' asked Propr, manipulating his moustache into a question mark.

'Let's leave grammar out of it for the moment,' said Jim turning his solemn face from Propr and settling his gaze on Lao. 'My friend, you malign the will when you represent it as a junior partner, an engine, a machine, a cold and efficient thing, like the Prussian army. Take the will away from mankind and we have only a sleeping potential for civilisation. Will is the potential in action. If men and women don't get out of bed in the morning . . .'

'It's going to the loo that gets me out of bed in the morning,' sniggered Sam.

'Will you let me finish!' snapped Jim. 'You're ruining my rhythm.'

'Don't mind me,' said Sam, his face paling. 'You're clearly on a roll.'

'God knows why the food is taking so long,' said Jute.

'As I was saying, if people don't get out of bed in the morning . . .'

'On the right side or the left . . .' said Propr.

With a certain magnificence, Jim ignored the interruption.

'There would be no electricity, no cars, no services, no industry, no culture . . .'

'Most poets work in bed, don't they . . .?' put in Sam.

'No houses, no aeroplanes, no food, no society. They would just be a people with no sense of their potential. A people we could justly call primitive . . .'

'I'm starving. Do you think the kitchen has forgotten us?' said Husk.

'Would you call them primitive because they don't get out of bed in the morning or because they do?' asked Propr.

'And do they have beds?' added Sam.

'These questions are irrelevant,' said Jim. 'But when a civilisation loses its will, as I think ours has, or when its will is corrupted, as with Rome, then the Barbarians will overcome it and give rise to new civilisations with the force of their will. You can interrupt me as much as you want, but the truth remains. In culture, industry, science, or warfare, will rules, will conquers, will overcomes. Pass the wine, somebody, for my will has run dry.'

CHAPTER 15

They all laughed nervously. But when the laughter subsided they looked at him in silence. They were also struck by a change in him. He had always been a mild-mannered man, but now a demonic force seemed to have quite banished the mildness. A curious power radiated from him.

Only Lao seemed bemused. He waited a moment before speaking.

CHAPTER 16

During that moment Jim underwent another subtle metamorphosis. A brooding air settled around him like a black cape. His eyes became haunted. He had deployed a lot of will in expounding upon the will, and he was drained but defiant. He appeared to be staring with vacant intensity at black holes in the air.

'That was a Faustian hymn, with some echoes of the Nuremberg rally,' said Lao quietly.

There were gasps of shock around the table. Jim only shrugged.

'It was a hymn to the will, an encomium, and taken to its logical conclusion could lead us to some pretty unpalatable places,' Lao went on into the expectant silence. 'It is interesting that, in the bible, individual will was the cause of man's fall.'

Lao paused. His voice got quieter and yet each word spoken was clear as the sound of a bell across the lake.

'There is something higher and more powerful than will. It is more fundamental as a civilising force. It contains will, but is greater. And it is indestructible.'

At that moment the waitress, helped by kitchen staff, brought in their various dishes. The aroma of sautéed potatoes, fried chicken, lightly grilled sirloin steak, filled the air. There was a general silence as each person received their food; silence, except for the moving of cutlery and glasses to make space for the salads, the fries, the oblong plates of *wienerschnitzel*, and the round plates on which lay steamed trout and sea-bass, their skins intact, their eyes glazed. When the waitress retreated, having filled their glasses with wine, they turned to Lao. But it was Propr who gave voice to the general expectation.

'Well, what is it? It's not a cheap answer like love, is it?'

'What's wrong with love?' said Husk.

'Nothing,' replied Propr. 'Only I'm fed up with it being the answer to everything. If that's the answer I think I'll explode.'

'Me too,' said Sam. 'What is this mysterious quality that is greater than will then? It's not freedom, is it?'

'I like freedom,' piped in Riley unexpectedly.

'I bet you do,' Sam said. 'Everyone wants to be free; and the freer they are the more unfree they become.'

'That can't be true,' said Jute.

'The freest person I ever saw,' said Sam, 'was a madman in the streets of Accra. He could do anything he wanted. He pissed on oranges in the marketplace. He insulted everybody. He said

102

anything he liked. But I didn't envy him one bit. Freedom is harder to handle than power, more existential than love. Too much freedom is spoiling us. It's the most overrated . . .'

'We're not talking about freedom, we're talking about will,' said Jute, bluntly. 'Let's eat, shall we . . .?'

They began eating, and while they ate and drank they all looked at Lao, waiting for him to announce the quality that was greater than will.

They all waited, except Mistletoe. She went on drawing, stopping long enough, now and then, to fork up a piece of sea-bass. She knew Lao's perversity, and had come to understand the reasoning behind it. They had talked about it often in the long conversations they had in bed in the mornings. In those conversations all aspects of life were their inspiration. They had talked about how, in the heat of a discussion, when people are pressing you to answer a question, it is often better not to do so. In the middle of a passionate debate people tend not to hear what is being said, and they have an inclination to disagree. Lao felt it was better if people could hear what was being said indirectly, for the deepest hearing happens long after the listening, and listening often awakens resistance.

'It's easier to be clever than to listen,' Lao said on one of those mornings.

'It took me more than a decade to hear something my father told me,' Mistletoe replied.

'It can take a lifetime.'

'We really hear long after we have heard. We hear best in recollection.'

'The best hearing is when the original words are resurrected in another experience, echoing through time . . .' Mistletoe went on quietly drawing, thinking about this with a smile.

'You still haven't answered,' Sam said to Lao at last. 'Come on. What is the quality that's greater than will?'

'Yes, you've had long enough to think of something. I've nearly finished my steak,' said Propr.

They were clearly frustrated by Lao's silence. Mistletoe, smiling still, knew that Lao was allowing the mood to thicken, increasing everyone's annoyance, the better to turn the mystery. People are surprisingly impervious, Lao often contended, and strategies of cunning simplicity are required to make them hear.

While they waited, he sat silently. Then Jim, finishing his *wienerschnitzel*, said:

'Lao needs a lifetime to come up with something. Sadly, we can't wait that long.'

'I don't need any time at all,' Lao retorted. 'What I want to say can be said in one word. It can even be demonstrated. In fact, the demonstration has already begun; this journey to Arcadia is the demonstration, and what will endure of it will be the proof.' He smiled cheekily. 'But my actual verbal answer will be given to an apparently unrelated question while you are all looking the other way.'

104

'You're just perverse,' said Jim.

'Absolutely,' said Lao.

'You're infuriating,' said Husk.

'I know.'

'You're a tease,' said Riley.

Lao shrugged.

'You haven't got an answer, you're just bluffing,' said Propr.

'Maybe, maybe not.'

'Don't indulge him,' said Jim. 'Ignore him. And ignore the other one too.'

'Who's the other one?' asked Lao. 'Oh, I know.'

'Who?' said Husk. And then, 'Oh, yes, I know too.'

'We all know,' said Propr.

'Can you please not mention that name?' said Jute. 'I want to sleep tonight.'

'I think we have invested that name with too much power,' said Lao. An uneasy silence fell over them. 'More than that,' Lao went on in the silence, 'we've somehow created him, and now we're becoming the victims of our own creation.'

'He's real enough,' said Jim solemnly. 'He's the one who assembled us for this journey.'

'Have you met him?' asked Lao.

'No.'

'Have you seen him?'

'No.'

'Do you have any physical proof that he exists?'

'You have as much proof as any of us – the notes, messages, communications . . .'

'They're not proof.'

'I've seen him,' said Jute. 'In glimpses.'

'Where?'

'On the journey, in mirrors, here and there.'

'Figments of your imagination.'

'I've had glimpses of him too,' said Husk.

'Me too,' said Riley.

'Me too,' said Sam.

'I still say we've made him up,' said Lao.

'How do you mean?' asked Jim.

'You know,' ventured Lao. 'He's a group entity.'

'What's that?' asked Jute.

'Something spectral that a group of people create among themselves.'

'How do they do it?' asked Riley in a tiny voice.

'With their minds,' said Lao. 'He's a creation of our minds.'

They waited for him to go on.

'Explain!' said Propr.

'There's nothing to explain,' said Lao.

'I don't like where this conversation is going,' said Jute.

'No, you're wrong' said Jim. 'He's real. He's not something created by our minds. If it weren't for him we wouldn't be on this journey. He's the guiding figure of our adventure.'

'He is a creation of our minds,' repeated Lao. 'The sooner we admit it, the better. Besides, a creation of the group mind can be more powerful than an actual person.'

'Powerful how?' said Riley.

'And in a good way or a bad way?' Propr added.

'It depends on the group. If our underlying dynamic is evil, the force we create will be evil. If it's good, the force will be benign,' said Lao.

'Are you making this up?' asked Sam.

'Don't listen,' Jim said. 'Don't let him spook you with all that mind stuff. The person we're talking about is real.'

'I'm easy about it all anyway,' said Lao. 'Everyone must live in accordance with their own light or darkness.'

A shadow seemed to fall over them and those still eating picked at their food a little disconsolately. They listened to the whisperings of the mountain wind. Then, one by one, they went up to their rooms.

BOOK IV

A LITTLE NIGHT MAGIC

CHAPTER 1

Lao and Mistletoe did not feel like sleeping just yet. Being in a new town was a call to adventure. They stayed in their room long enough to change into more informal clothes. Then they stole out of the hotel to find what entertainment the small town offered.

They walked down the road that ran alongside the lake. The mountain loomed in the dark, unseen. Bright clusters of towns, rising tier upon tier, dazzled from the other side of the lake. To their right was the distant Klewenalp.

As they walked they heard music. It seemed to come from the lake. Lao, thinking about the lake and the mountain, said:

'A lake's mystery depends upon her surroundings.'

'What do you mean?'

'If a lake is surrounded by forest . . .'

'It takes on the quality of a fairy tale.'

'But if it's at the foot of a mountain . . .'

'It becomes sublime.'

They walked on in silence. They found, without knowing when, that they had turned off the road and wandered towards the town. The essence of pine was carried from the mountain on the swift wind. Elegant houses, of wood and stone, appeared dimly in the faint light. They had read that the mountains had given rise to legends of dragons and giants, ghosts and witches and even meerkats. Something of those legends scented the air as they wandered through the quiet streets, following their intuition.

Everything they saw was wrapped in the mystery of first encounters. They stared at gardens and school buildings, at darkened restaurants and shop-windows and little parks. They knew they were not seeing what was there but only the strangeness and the general beauty of the new place. They had often talked about this in the past, in fact they had abbreviated it to a formula: *to see something once you need to see it thrice*. But they also felt that first seeing had something special about it and they tried to be attentive to the revelations and misunderstandings of first encounters, with books, people and places.

They walked through the dream-like streets of the town, aware that they were idealising it. Quaint buildings, like dolls' houses, were simplified by their gaze. A fairy tale mood accompanied them through the sleeping town. The night invested everything with a quality from another realm. The strangeness made them alert.

They passed a dimly lit blue and yellow post office, wooden chalets and stone houses. A clock tower stood mute in the centre of a street. They couldn't read the time on its face. The statue of a boy interrupted them. It seemed as if everything was stripped of its original intention and now stood in the dark, like signposts in a world of dreams.

Lao was gliding through a world he knew before birth. Mistletoe was in a lucid dream. The wind was gentle, the air pure and lovely to breathe. Each breath felt like a purification.

Things which we experience for the first time and which delight us are glimpses of Eden, Lao thought. The beauty of first encounters is so fleeting. The wise wait for time to recast its spell before returning to those encounters again.

'We're not coming back here for a long time, if ever,' he said aloud.

'How do you know?'

'I feel it.'

'Then we should really take it in while we're here.'

'But can we?'

'We can try.'

'The first time will be the best, though,' said Lao.

'I don't know,' Mistletoe said. 'There's wisdom in repetition, in going to the same place often, seeing the same painting again and again, re-reading a much loved book.'

'Most people would say repetition is boring.'

'The young maybe.'

'We're young,' Lao laughed briefly. 'I think the first seeing, the first mis-reading is the truest.'

'Why? You didn't think so before. You used to say thrice is once.'

'I still do. But I think something of our deeper selves lives in the magic of first encounters. We try later to recapture that first enchantment, but only rare experiences reawaken it.'

'Maybe we'll awaken the magic of this walk in a future journey.'

'I suppose that's what a classic is.'

'What?'

'A work that has the spring of eternal freshness within it. It manages to be new each time you encounter it.'

'Yes,' Mistletoe said. 'But some time needs to pass for the magic to be renewed.'

With wonder and breath-held silence, they went through the streets as if they were tiptoeing through the room of a sleeping child. They would have liked to get lost in the town, lost in its mood, because reality is the greatest misunderstanding of them all.

CHAPTER 2

Mistletoe had a sudden uncertain premonition. She was about to say something about Malasso when Lao pointed to the lights of a pub in the middle of a lane.

They stepped into its roar like waking from a dream. Loud drunken conversations crowded the smoky air and a rock anthem thundered from the jukebox. Dark walls were plastered with fading posters of dancing girls, music concerts, and festivals. The place smelled of spilt beer.

Faces turned as Lao and Mistletoe walked in. Lao felt the gazes returning him to the world of colour, as if the air was suddenly charged. Amid the smoke he felt the weight of a mute judgement. It was as if their presence in the pub had contravened some unspoken law.

Lao and Mistletoe stopped and looked round, assessing the quality of the mood, feeling for its dangers. For a long moment, in spite of the anthemic roar from the jukebox, silence seemed to prevail.

Deciding that what one decrees from within is what the world sees in you, and at that moment happening to see himself as a prince from an infinite kingdom, Lao regained the integrity of his being. He cast a protective spell around Mistletoe, as she cast one around him.

So they strode into the depths of the pub like enchanters, altering reality by altering themselves. All at once they seemed like regulars who had been away for a long time. They went to the counter and ordered two pints of the local beer and looked around, as if they were curious about the new faces they saw leaning against the walls, standing in clusters, darkening the ceiling with smoke.

CHAPTER 3

Lao engaged one of the bartenders in conversation. He asked about the copper tankards that were ranged on shelves along the walls according to their sizes. Etched on the side of some was the figure of a goat-footed man, on others a noble stag. The barman told him that every year, on midsummer nights, they had drinking competitions in the open air. The winner, in addition to their prize, got to drink from a tankard. It was a tradition that went back a thousand years. But this year the winner had been a complete unknown; and when he won he had disappeared back to where he came from without drinking from the winner's tankard or collecting his prize, like a figure from a fairy tale.

'What was the prize?' Lao asked.

The barman gave an obscene leer.

'It's a secret. Only the mayor knows.'

The publican had to go and serve someone. Mistletoe and Lao drank their beer in silence, leaning against the counter.

The pub had changed its mind about them.

CHAPTER 4

They soon discovered a pool table at the back of the pub. On the walls there were dusty swords, ancient poignards, muskets, an armorial shield, and the stuffed head of a stag with branching antlers.

To their surprise, among the players they saw their driver, Bruno the Second. He was coming to the end of a game with one of the bulky denizens of the establishment. Bruno was not surprised to see them.

'I knew you two would turn up here sooner or later,' he said.

He seemed different from the fresh-faced young man who had driven them from Basel station to their hotel. He seemed more himself.

'I'm glad you came. We're not having a very good game. This man is a lazy player – don't worry, he doesn't speak English. Would you like to play? A bet would be nice, don't you think?'

Lao was immediately interested. He liked the occasional gamble, though he hadn't played pool in years and was very rusty. But he was fond of it, the sociability it called for, the concentration it demanded, the precision it required. It was a game of courage and canniness, risk and rhythm, intuition and intelligence. He enjoyed its theatricality. Being upset when beaten and generous in victory were part of its pleasures. The game offered him scope to express both his villainy and his heroism.

Bruno dispatched his mediocre challenger, invigorated by the new arrivals. With a cocky air he racked up the balls and chalked his cue stick. He and Lao agreed on a bet, just big enough to compel concentration.

'I'm at a disadvantage,' Lao said.

'How?' asked Bruno. 'Because you're black?'

Lao looked at him and smiled. It had been said with warmth, with innocence even. That made all the difference.

'No,' Lao said. 'Because my woman is here. There is more pressure on me.'

'Oh, I see. Can't afford to lose, eh?'

'Something like that.'

'It's easier to lose if you have to win.'

Lao shrugged. He had been lying. He knew he could lose a thousand times and Mistletoe would put it in context with a phrase. She made herself invisible to Lao. The pressure was on Bruno, but Bruno didn't know it.

CHAPTER 5

Bruno won the break. The game progressed, and the crowd of on-lookers grew. They brought their murmurs, their side bets, and their cigarette smoke. Bruno played to the limit of his limitation.

He talked while he played. Lao liked him the more he listened.

'All my life I have wanted to be a doctor. I have one more year to go. I want to go to Africa, to help the poor and the sick. I am doing two other jobs besides being your driver. My father was an engineer. Now he's retired. He worked in Africa. Maybe you know him. My mother is a teacher. It's because of her I speak English. Is my English good?'

Lao nodded.

'Thank you. I was born near Basel, but all my life I have dreamt of going to Africa. I don't know why. All my school-mates used to read books about America or mountain climbers or racing-car drivers, but I read everything I could about Africa. Isn't that strange? I have never been there, but I feel in a way African. Can I say that?'

Lao shrugged again.

'Why not?' he said encouragingly.

Bruno paused in his play. He had been playing formidably well. He gave Lao a long thoughtful look. Then he said:

'This feeling I have for Africa is one of the greatest mysteries of my life.'

Lao wasn't sure what to say, so he stayed silent. He had met people with a nostalgia for Africa. Most of them had never been to the continent, but said they had Africa in their souls. Some of them spoke of Africa as a place they had known; it was a place in them older than memory. Reincarnation was a subject Lao seldom discussed. To know something means needing no explanation and having no need to explain to others. Life is coloured by such knowledge. To know one thing is to know many others. To know is to be silent. Lao never spoke of such things. Instead, he played. Bruno had lost a shot, and it was Lao's turn.

CHAPTER 6

Having not played the game for a while, Lao had no sense of his limitations. To his mild surprise he potted balls he would normally have missed even before he'd played them. In the past, faced with such shots, he would fear that he couldn't pocket the ball. More often than not, it worked out as he feared.

In the past, before a game began, Lao always knew whether he would win or lose. Often, leaning towards a lazy fatalism, he knew deep down that he would lose; but he would play for fun, and lose anyway. Then he would feel bad. The bad feeling, stored away for the next game, made him feel he would lose again.

Then sometimes when he won it was in spite of himself. When he thought about it, though, he realised that when he won it was usually because he was absorbed in the game, engaged but detached, and that natural flow made him victorious. He found that he could determine the outcome from one moment to another if he danced with the nature of his opponent's game, playing as if in a dream.

CHAPTER 7

In the past, Lao estimated his chance of victory or defeat on how well his opponent played. But he sometimes found that he was victorious even when his opponent was many times better than him. And when he thought about it, he came to the conclusion that there are three levels of skill: the actual, the real, and the amplified. The actual skill is the game as one plays it normally: it is apparent. The real skill emerges in the negative spaces of the game: it is one's potential. Amplified skill, superior to the others, is akin to perpetual inspiration. It is when a player is possessed by a higher force. To have all three levels consistently high is what makes a master. But genius plays the infinite game.

Then there is the game of reality, and the reality of the game.

These were some nebulous fruits of Lao's meditations on his victories and defeats.

CHAPTER 8

For the first time in his life, inspired by an Arcadia growing in him, Lao played with no sense of limitation. He played with an enchanted freedom. It was as though he had left behind all his complicated baggage. It was curious that the new bud of tranquillity in him had found something so ordinary as a game of pool to reveal its powers.

He went round the green baize table, potting balls leisurely, inspired by the click of contact. He didn't soar, or experience an epiphany; he was no different from normal. He was just more himself than normal. He felt himself to be a truer Lao; and some mysterious picture he had of himself was clearer.

As he played he was dimly aware of the faces watching them, of the smell of beer, and the pop song on the jukebox. With clean shots he potted a blue ball, then a red, then a yellow. The balls dropped into the pocket with a maternal sound.

For a moment he was aware also of the mountains around them. He glimpsed the dream that lurked in the heart of reality. He felt both in the present and eternal. For a moment, he was his fact and his fantasy. He had already decided the outcome of the game, and was merely toying with the route by which to get there.

By then, the atmosphere in the pub was electric, presided over by the stag's head. Bruno kept twirling his cue stick between his palms. Lao kept on winning. Mistletoe noticed the unusual gleam in one of his eyes and included it in the sketch she had been making of the two of them. She had never drawn people playing pool before, and this was a unique opportunity. She drew the faces round the table, hinted at the smoky atmosphere; even the stag's head found a place in her drawing.

While pondering a shot Lao found himself staring at that head. He had a sudden vision of a magnificent stag high on a rock in the dark mountain. His mind wandered for a second. When he took the shot he missed the pocket and found he had lost his Arcadian mood. He began to play badly. He lost game after game. Then Bruno, prancing round the table, put the balls away with a vengeance, and caught up with him in the scores.

It occurred to Lao that, on the whole, people don't change. He hadn't changed. He had the same bad habits of mind. We are like layers of rock, he thought, and our true self is covered over with strata of experience, habit, education, ideology. The true person is in there, somewhere. Can it be awoken? I was once a magnificent stag high up on the mountaintop. Can I be that stag again?

This thought came as a shock to Lao, but he didn't have time to think it through. The game was coming to an end and he was losing. To make matters worse, Bruno had him snookered.

CHAPTER 9

At that moment Lao also had a premonition of Malasso. He sensed his presence in the night, and it made him shiver. Then it occurred to him, as he got ready to take the shot from his snookered position, that a tincture of evil aids excellence. The evil faces from history rose up in his mind. He allowed them to summon a force of opposition in him. From the air he stole the power of heroes. He succeeded in his shot, and played with a new concentration. A gem-like toughness compacted itself in him.

It was at this point that Bruno made his gravest error. He sidled across to Mistletoe and gave her drawing his intense concentration.

'What is this?' he asked, charmingly. 'Ah, such a beautiful drawing! You are making art as we play? You make your friend look too serious, no? I like the stuffed stag. Very realistic. You have beauty and talent, yes?'

Bruno continued in this way in a friendly voice just as Lao was contemplating a difficult shot. It was a ricochet blue into the middle pocket from an awkward angle. Lao frowned. It seemed the attention Bruno was paying Mistletoe was working.

But Bruno did not know that between some people exists the original Enochian language, the ability to speak to each other in spirit. He did not know what had been forged between these two people, forged through time, gnosis, and their mutual commitment to the highest things in life.

Bruno did not know that Mistletoe saw through him and thought it shabby that he was playing Iago to Lao's concentration.

She did something curious. She included Bruno in the sketch, placed him in a net of rough lines, and on his back she heaped rocks and around him she drew the dark women of mythology, Lilith, the lamia, the medusa.

Bruno, noticing that Lao was fighting his distraction, leant towards Mistletoe again.

'A beautiful artist and a beautiful woman . . .' he murmured.

But when he looked at the drawing again, he froze.

Mistletoe, in a soft voice, said, 'I think a lesson is called for.'

Lao may or may not have heard. But he smiled. Reaching for an obscure evil in him, and converting it into skill, the ricochet was executed, and the ball returned to its home. The rest of the shots followed from an amplified clarity of spirit. The balls sank into the pockets smoothly.

He returned the cue to its stand. He shook

Bruno's hand, collected his winnings and, with a nod to Mistletoe, went past the crowd, to the outer chamber of the pub.

On his way out the barman called him over.

'You are like the man in the drinking competition,' he said.

Lao shrugged. The barman touched him affectionately on the shoulder.

'This is a strange town,' he said confidentially.

'Is it safe?' Lao asked.

'Yes, of course. But interesting things happen here.'

'Like what?'

'People see things.'

'I'll be careful.'

'Would you like to drink from a tankard to celebrate?'

'Another time, perhaps.'

The barman gave him a knowing smile. It half occurred to Lao that the town was enchanted, but he shook the thought from his mind, and went out into the dark.

CHAPTER 10

Not long afterwards Mistletoe joined him. Not one word was said about the game. They wandered in silence into the midsummer night and made their way back up the lane. They passed the quaint buildings that were like giant dolls' houses and they thought about fairy tales, trolls, and wizards guarding treasures. Dreams floated past them in the dark.

Reality can be altered by the mind, Lao thought. All it takes is the right magic, the right attitude. Whoever knows this secret never fails.

They turned into the road and saw in the dark ahead of them a playground. The seesaw was tilted heavenward, and the swing twisted lightly. Mistletoe noticed how curious the playground was when there were no children and when only the night played there, along with silent forms.

In the distance they saw a bridge, faintly lit. It looked as if it went from darkness to nowhere. They walked towards it, without purpose, drawn by the fairy tales lingering in the air. Beyond were lights that changed, that summoned.

The darkness was alive with intangible forms.

They came to a little woodland and Lao stopped walking. There were ideas that had come to him during the game that he wanted to think about. He couldn't quite remember what they were.

He stood still and gazed at the stars in the sky. They seemed to move. He wanted to go beyond thought. He wanted things to settle in him and find their place. He also wanted to let go of old ways of being.

But Mistletoe wanted the dark. While Lao gazed at Ursa Minor, she wandered on alone, towards the bridge.

She went soundlessly past the fragrance of honeysuckle. She went into the substance of night, till her own substance was dissolved in it.

Lao stood there near the woodland, not thinking. He felt himself returning to some primal condition and lost all sense of who he was, or what he was. He was not thinking but listening to intimate whisperings. He was listening to the music of flowers. He felt he had entered an invisible temple that drifts through time. He could feel the earth revolving.

He was not aware that Mistletoe had gone.

CHAPTER 11

Mistletoe had wandered into her own eternity. In the darkness she found freedom from her body and from endless watching eyes. When she was under the bridge she looked back and saw only the blackness of night but was not afraid. She walked into the marmorial darkness.

As she passed beneath the darkness of the bridge she passed into her own legendary world. She saw a huge white horse in a field of blue flowers. Then the horse disappeared.

She came to a field. In the middle of the field was a circus. The music of pipes and strings and drums pervaded the warm summer night. Performers were rehearsing in the artificial moonlight that poured from an opalescent globe. The dancers did their stretches, the jugglers practised with their seven balls, and knife throwers slung their knives at revolving targets.

Women in red and yellow outfits rode on unicycles, balancing a stack of books on their heads. Women in golden dresses stood on the backs of horses, white birds on their outstretched hands.

Under the glow of a Chinese lantern a girl wrapped in the universal flag of imagination wielded a starry wand. With the wand she turned a furry fruit into a rabbit, the rabbit into a bird, the bird into an angel, the angel into a star, and she sent the star into the sky, where it twinkled merrily. Mistletoe smiled at the girl as she went past. The girl looked at her, puzzled.

Mistletoe watched a harlequin execute somersaults through hoops of coloured lights. A black girl dressed like a Valkyrie flew around in the air and swooped down through a triangle of fire, singing.

Nearby there was a blue tent with the sign of the pentagram. The door flap opened and a magician with milk-white eyes came out. The magician wore a white suit and a black top hat, and carried a cane whose upper section had two entwined snakes. But the magician, turning around, became a beautiful woman in a blue suit with a pentagram wand. She danced over to Mistletoe, and said:

'We thought you'd never show up.'

CHAPTER 12

Mistletoe, surprised that she had been expected, felt the heat of an inexplicable fire above her head.

The magician in the blue suit with the different back led Mistletoe to the centre of the field. Then she clapped her hands together three times, and said:

'Hey, daughters of Pan, guess who's here.'

The harlequin stopped somersaulting, and landed in perfect balletic balance. The conjuror allowed a dove to circle the air untransformed. The girls riding the horses leapt down, and the flying black girl dropped gracefully into their midst. Soon the jugglers, knife throwers, unicyclists and dancers had all gathered round in a circle. They stared and then, as if in sudden recognition, one of them cried:

'It's Mistletoe!'

'It's our Mistletoe!' said another.

'We thought we'd never see you again.'

'We thought you'd forgotten us.'

Then they clustered round her, welcoming their sister back to their enchanted world.

'Perform for us!' the conjuror cried.

'But what shall I do?' Mistletoe asked.

The innocence of the question made them laugh. Mistletoe still looked perplexed. Then the magician touched her on the head with the pentagram wand and Mistletoe remembered what her special talent was in that world.

A large white canvas stood before her. The conjuror gave Mistletoe her wand. Without thinking, as if she had been doing this all her life, Mistletoe began drawing figures on the magic canvas. The figures, as if emerging from mirrors, fell out of the canvas and became real. She drew a white horse and it galloped round the field. She sketched a flute and gave it to the black girl. She drew bottles of champagne and passed them round. She inscribed the outlines of a book, and someone asked what it was called.

'You suggest,' Mistletoe said.

'Astonishing the Gods,' the magician replied.

Mistletoe wrote out the title, and gave it to her. The daughters of Pan applauded. Then Mistletoe wrote the words: MUST GO NOW. And they all said, 'No! Stay with us!'

Mistletoe wrote on the canvas: I LOVE YOU ALL.

'We love you too,' they replied.

Then she wrote: ARCADIA.

And they clapped their hands, and said, 'We'll see you there!'

Mistletoe stopped drawing and returned the wand to the conjuror. The circus folk gathered round and hugged her. They led her to the edge of the field of blue flowers and the magician tapped her on the head with the pentagram wand.

Mistletoe found herself beneath the bridge, where it was darkest. An illusive melody in her head accompanied her past the fragrance of honeysuckle, when she regained her substance from the riches of the night.

CHAPTER 13

He had been searching for her up and down the street. He had ventured towards the bridge but thought it unlikely that she had gone into its darkness. He had been beginning to be frantic, fearing he had somehow lost her forever. Then he decided to be still, and to wait. But his anger and his fear remained.

He was standing where she had left him, and he still appeared to be gazing at the stars. But his profile communicated to her a sense of estrangement.

Upon seeing him she knew he had been worried. She wanted to tell him how much she needed a little renewal. I have to keep overcoming myself in order to love more fully, she thought, as she drew closer to him. How can I not breathe the secret hour if it will enrich me?

Lao stood in the shadow of the woodland, and turned his head slightly in her direction, and she knew that he was still upset. But a woman should have her mysteries, Mistletoe thought, and they should be mysterious even to herself. As she got near him she sensed his conflicting emotions. Loving or eviling, she thought. Which would win?

From experience she knew that any gesture she made might worsen his mood. She gave him a severe little smile. Then she went past him quietly. She went on down the street. The architect of the dark had redesigned all the houses with night-substance.

Most places look better and truer at night, she thought. She came to a solitary street lamp. Finding herself in the centre of the light, she turned and saw Lao walking towards her. He had a contemplative look.

She went on into the darkness, and waited for him, with a question in her mind. When he stood in the ghostly pool of light, alone in a theatre of night, she began speaking to him. She reminded him of something he had written a long time ago. He had written that in dreams the mind is the stage, and the play staged upon it is our drama, already scripted in the book of life.

As he listened a shiver ran through him.

'If that's the case,' continued Mistletoe, 'then the people in our dreams are all us. The places are us. The meaning is us too. We are the message, and we can change the dream. We can alter the script.'

She paused. Disturbed by an intimation whose source is dream-like, he stood rooted in the theatre of light.

'You said if we can't change the beginning we can change the end. If we can't change the end we can change the middle while dreaming and so change the meaning of the end. But something bothers me.'

Lao stayed silent. He was struck by the way the night altered the tone of her voice and the implication of her words.

'If the stage is us, and all the people in the dream are us, and the dream is our drama, why are we watching?'

'Because we're the audience too,' said Lao, seduced by the game.

'Why do we need an audience then?'

'Because we learn by doing and remembering what we do. There's a watcher in us keeping an eye on the dream-drama in our minds. We don't know who that watcher is.'

Lao paused for a moment. He was dissatisfied with his answer and conscious of her silence. He made another attempt.

'We only play one role in life. We're either the participant or the spectator. In dreams we're both at the same time. Maybe this speeds up our understanding. The participant experiences more. The spectator sees more. The participant is sometimes wrong: they experience only their own point of view. The spectator is also wrong sometimes: they don't have responsibility, they can witness without risking anything, learn without suffering. But the two together – taking part and watching – maybe that's what produces the true history of our lives.'

He paused again. Mistletoe had moved a little closer to him.

'You're saying that dreams are our rehearsal for life,' said Mistletoe.

'Like private plays.'

'So plays we see in real theatres are private dreams shown in public?'

'One person's consciousness, read by the universe . . .'

'Bearing witness to all of us.'

'Maybe there's a spiritual black box in us that is decoded when we die.'

'So books should be lived to be read.'

'And life should be dreamt to be lived.'

Lao laughed. 'You've got me talking,' he said. 'What are you hiding? I feel like a bomb that's been delicately defused. Where did you go? What are you trying to divert me from?'

'Only from how much I love you,' said Mistletoe, joining him in the pool of light.

CHAPTER 14

They made their way back to the hotel through the gentle darkness of the town. Near the clock tower, a night-bird flew low overhead. The whirring of its wings reminded them of something ethereal, something they used to know but couldn't now remember. They were a little tired.

In an obscure way they felt they were being initiated into a new reality. They had become fond of the night-town, and had made it a small part of themselves. They felt they had become part of the town too, part of its dreams. In the town's black box would be recorded the fact that they had been there. They had breathed deeply there, and hadn't merely passed through. They liked to think that its night would always recognise them.

CHAPTER 15

Lao was struck by Mistletoe's strangeness on her return from the place beyond the bridge. There was an alien sensuality about her, something new that awed and aroused him, even scared him a little. She seemed transformed. She seemed, in some way, magnified.

As they made their way back, breathing deeply the lake and mountain air, he kept glancing at her, but she was silent.

CHAPTER 16

As Mistletoe dressed for bed she became aware of a change. Her mouth was dry, her breathing awkward, her heartbeat irregular. Her hands quivered lightly and she felt as if she had a mild fever. Curious colours swam in her eyes. She felt a little dizzy.

She slipped into bed, and listened to Lao's breathing in the dark. A dark red heat poured from him. She noticed that he was lying heavier on the bed beside her.

When his hand brushed her nipple it tripped a switch and she came alight. He touched her belly and his hand seemed to burn through her. He lavished on her body indirect touches and bitter-sweet sensations flooded her brain.

She became aware of places in her that could only have been concealed there by a god with a sense of humour. Adrift on warm currents, no longer of this world, she became aware of him gliding into her. He loved her with gentleness and strength, stroking her neck, praising her face with his hands, till she was broken up and began a low rhythmic wail. She was a little overwhelmed with being the adored focus of such power, as he rose and fell. She felt certain now that there was a heaven and that it was here, in her body. The universe was in her and with each movement it unfolded to her.

Somewhere in the night a stray rocket went off. She must have been shouting, for his hand was cupping her mouth. Lost to all reason, she wanted to encompass him with beautiful obscenities.

She suddenly learnt surrender, and broke through all her barriers, and destroyed his control. In an ecstasy greater than his anguish, he raced towards her, and disappeared into her universe, and afterwards into a long dreamless slumber.

BOOK V

A SHADOWY PRESENCE

*T*he alchemy of Arcadia worked on the group in unexpected ways. Malasso was one of those ways. Had they all created him? Was it true that he was a group entity? Whatever he was, they had empowered him. They endowed him with influence, nourished his personality, enriched his agency. They made him the deity of their journey. Through their fears, fantasies, secrets, and undefined creativity they made him a minor demiurge.

He grew with their breath. Their thoughts filled out his insubstantial form. Their desires were his gains. He acquired might from their floating dreams. Moving between two realms, he was both visible and invisible. Mirroring their blind alternation between dream and waking, thought and things, he became the master between – the master they had brought with them. With their ungoverned wishes they gave him the key to their destinies on the journey.

Unwittingly they conferred on him the power to shape their stories: he could influence whatever happened to them as they travelled through the myth-charged spaces to Arcadia.

His powers grew as their thoughts intensified. Through

them he was now clothed in pure energy. As they were, so was he. When they were negative, he grew; when elevated, he flew. He sowed mischief with their weakest thoughts; he amplified such thoughts, made them real, and gave each fantasy a form.

He was their ambiguous genie. And because his power came from their hidden source, he was a monarch of their minds. Darkness and sunlight were to him equal nourishment.

CHAPTER 1

After dinner, Jim called on Sam to inspect the results of the filming so far and to plan the work of the coming days. Sam was exhausted and a bit drunk and had been reading his Camus in bed when Jim came by. They talked about the helicopter shots planned for the next day, views of the mountain capped with snow and mist. Sam was particularly looking forward to the challenge of dangling upside down, in harness, while filming.

On his way back to his room, Jim stopped at Husk's room. She was talking to someone in London and abruptly slammed down the phone and burst into tears on Jim's shoulder. But she quickly pulled herself together. She made no explanation of the phone call or the tears as they went through the logistics of the next day's filming, the hiring of the helicopter and van, and the provisions needed. When he was satisfied that everything was in hand, Jim asked if she needed help and Husk assured him that she was fine. She led him to the door with a thin smile, and shut it after him.

Jim went to his room but, finding that he felt agitated, he decided to go out for a walk along the silver shores of the lake. He needed the walk. Underneath his efficiency, Jim was troubled by the latter part of the conversation at dinner. The talk about Malasso had been niggling away at him. He had not liked the idea of a shadowy presence hovering over the group, haunting them in diverse ways. He had particularly not liked the notion of this shadowy figure being a group entity, created by the sum total of the underlying attitudes and negative energies of the group.

The lake shone in the dark. It made him think of Avalon and the magic lake from which came the sword Excalibur, and to which it returned. The mountain was indistinguishable from the night. It was the quality of night which gave the lake its shimmer. As he stared at the lake Jim had a keen desire to leap into it, to sink right to the bottom and rest there. Perhaps he would find the lady of the lake and she might have a spell to cleanse him of his troubles.

The impulse to leap into the lake and rest in its depths was a strong one, and it surprised him. For when he examined it he found that it was a covert desire for death.

He had gone quite far on his walk, past a pier and some illuminated boats, when he heard a voice. It was a sweet and airy voice. Had someone called out his name? He saw no one. The darkness suddenly became sinister. Then he heard the voice

150

again, faint, distant, seeming to rise from the lake itself. He turned round and hurried in the direction of the hotel, horribly aware of something following in his shadow, something that glided, and whispered, but which vanished when he turned round. He began to run, and felt a cloaked form above him and glimpsed in his panic a masked face. He was glad when he made it through the front door of the hotel.

Back in his room, the door firmly shut, he conceded that there might be something to the notion of a group entity. He didn't think Malasso was that entity. Malasso was quite real to him.

CHAPTER 2

Jim tried to sleep, but couldn't. His mind was agitated. He was annoyed with himself for having revealed to Lao the story of his encounter with the Devil. He couldn't understand why he had done that. And had it happened to him, had it been an elaborate life-like dream, or had the encounter itself, so fantastic to the conscious mind, taken on an imaginative quality to protect him from the reality of it? He had been drawn into talking about it by a mood that had been taking possession of him, a mood that got worse the further they advanced on the journey to Arcadia.

In the coach, during the long drive from Basel, he had, among other things, been engaged in the writing of a list. He found it soothing and cathartic to enumerate all the things he hated, all the things that made life unbearable. He found it helpful to compile such a list. It saved him from himself. It was a kind of purgation.

He had been making lists like that for a long time. The first list began in the years of his first failure. He had spent considerable time and energy making his first film, and when it sank in the quicksand of indifference, he began compiling a private list of the intolerable things in life. He developed a clear eye for humbug in modern society, for things that diminish the magic of living. After that, whenever he suffered a failure he consoled himself with an elaboration of his list. It grew to be very extensive. If he had had the rigour or leisure of a Bouvard or a Pécuchet, he might have compiled not a dictionary of received ideas, but a dictionary of negations.

While filming, wherever he found himself, whether in a hotel room or on a train, he expanded his list with the passion of a connoisseur. After his list-making, he would fall into a kind of reverie.

CHAPTER 3

The list he had made on the coach, which culminated in the words KILL MALASSO, was written as if under the influence of a malignant moon. He had written:

I hate people who are confident and who have everything worked out.
I can't stand smugness.
I can't stand young people who are cocky, and older people who are snobs.
I am infuriated by people who just happen to have umbrellas when it starts to rain.
I can't stomach people who are too happy, and who have perfect lives.
I can't stand the newly successful, the newly famous.
People with regular features are quite intolerable.
Tall men are tiresome.
Short confident men are exasperating.
The eager and the enthusiastic drive me to distraction.
Women with cold eyes give me the shivers . . .

But none of this was what he wanted to write.
Then he had written:

KILL MALASSO.

Then he had told Lao the story he had told no one else.

Since he had set out on the journey to Arcadia, instead of life becoming more harmonious, it had become more fierce.

CHAPTER 4

Unable to sleep, he felt that shadowy presence again. It was now in the room. Before long Jim found himself occupied by a mood alien to him, an eviling mood. But it couldn't have been so alien or it wouldn't have found a place in him.

The mood had much to feast on in his soul. It fed on his life-long timidity, his failures and resentments and envy. It fed on that bile that formed out of having lived most of his life below his potential. It fed on the success of others, on his secret cowardice.

He got out of bed and fetched his notebook. He had to get rid of his obsessions. His inwardly directed anger had to be turned outward, free at last to express itself instead of feeding on his entrails. He had to get the poisons out of himself, get them out in words, so he could see them. A list was the only thing that could help him sleep. It was a way of escaping his narrow condition. Then, a little relieved, he might find rest.

He lifted his pen and, with the shadowy presence

hovering over him, and the dream of Arcadia inside him, he began to write.

Things that make life intolerable

People with no patience.
Idealists, dreamers, fantasists.
Small towns.
People who pride themselves on their realism.
Materialists, mystics, atheists, agnostics.
Cynics like Lao.
Multinationals.
Dictators.
Blind belief in democracy.
Third world debts.
Ignorance.
Bad education.
Too much education.
Romantics.
The world weary.
People who judge only by past performance.
People without imagination.
People who don't make up their own minds,
  but are led like sheep.
People who believe everything they read or hear.
All those who don't love what they do.
People who don't like their lives, but dare not
  change it.
Manipulators.
Monopolies.
Malasso . . .

CHAPTER 5

Every such list is a narrowing of options. Every such list shows how it is no longer possible to live. The act of writing is an act of creation. Psychologists say that writing something down facilitates its fulfilment.

Without him knowing it, Jim's lists, accumulating from year to year, became increasingly more severe. Without knowing it, the lists bricked him in. They made his life prickly with contradictions. He was in effect writing himself out of the broad script of life. Rejecting so much, out of vengeance, he had turned against happiness in life. He was secretly at war with himself. No one would have suspected this.

Outwardly jovial and polite, never angry, incapable of a fine manly rage, the kind of rage that lets the world quiver for a moment at a potential for violence or genius, Jim was nice because he was scared.

Lao suspected what lay behind this soft-spoken aspect of Jim, and loved to ruffle it. But he never suspected what it concealed. Too much concealing of true feelings leads to their compression, to rage beneath rage, masks beneath masks. Only in his lists did Jim reveal the depth of his concealment.

His lists were never about what he loved, what he wanted.

He had made his life a mirror of dissatisfactions, a veil of evils, and that was why the journey to Arcadia appealed to him. He longed to pierce the veil of evils, to crack the mirror of dissatisfactions. He wanted to believe in something. He wanted to act, to make the world right. He wanted to love life again.

Then came Malasso – Malasso who distilled into his featureless power and malignity everything Jim ever felt trapped by. Then came Malasso – the manipulator of the last free act of which Jim felt capable. His film.

He became doubly obsessed: with the Arcadia journey, and with Malasso, its antithesis.

CHAPTER 6

With new inspiration, Jim felt that making lists wasn't enough any more.

When a man like Jim comes to the end of his list-making he has nothing left but suicide or murder, despair or action. Now that he had at last identified Malasso as the chief enemy of his work, Jim had come to the end of an old road and knew he must build a new one, or perish. That was probably why he spoke with such passion about will.

The alchemy of Arcadia was cooking him, driving him mad.

He must do something, or die of not doing. He must transcend Faust, and solve the enigma of the Devil.

CHAPTER 7

Jute had often dreamt of falling in love, and never had. She had been in a few relationships and had pretended to be in love, but had never really felt it. With time she had just stopped pretending. She withdrew into a shell of withered emotions. Before she knew it she had dried up and could no longer feel very much, not even the death of her mother with whom she had not been very close.

The drying up of her heart did not trouble her at first. She barely noticed it. An immensely practical person, she accepted herself as she was, and got on with things, and never complained. She didn't really care.

But sometimes, between activities, at her desk or walking home, she would suddenly stop what she was doing and stare into space till her eyes filled with tears.

These moments of unconscious weeping were becoming more frequent. They were becoming embarrassing. She would be at an editorial meeting, listening to programme proposals, when she would unexpectedly well up. Sometimes she didn't notice her own tears till someone asked if she was all right. Then she would have to rush to the ladies' to refresh herself.

It was as though she was not feeling what she was feeling; as though behind her back someone was working the wells of her emotions. Her boss had suggested she see a specialist, but she had refused for she believed nothing was wrong with her. She put it down to overwork. She put it down to many things.

One day the proposal for an Arcadia journey came up for discussion at the meeting. Jute was listening to the presentation when once again the tears began flowing.

'If you feel so strongly about this, you should take it on,' her boss said.

She hadn't been aware that she was weeping. She excused herself and by the time she got back from the ladies' it was decided. She hadn't chosen the journey, somehow it had chosen her. In fact, she despised the idea of the journey. She considered it sentimental. She would rather die than be sentimental.

CHAPTER 8

The oddest thing had happened to Jute that evening. She had fallen in love, instantly, with the owner of the hotel, Hans. She liked his genial face, his sparkling eyes, and his fine moustache. She liked his old-world, small-town good manners. When they arrived in the hotel foyer, when he smiled at her in what she thought of as a special manner, she felt something awaken in her that had not been there before.

She became shy in his admiring presence. She felt his eyes on her and felt warm all over and wanted to escape and wanted at the same time to stay there under his gaze. When she tried to speak her voice became a croak and her mouth turned dry.

Bewildered by her own feelings, she felt she had been bewitched.

CHAPTER 9

Like all truly adorable people, she did not
think herself beautiful. She wore ungainly
glasses to emphasise her plainness. It was
difficult to flatter her, so men found her formid-
able. They feared her before she feared them. This
was confirmed when they came up against the
solid brick wall of her personality.

Nothing impressed her. She was doughty,
impenetrable, unflappable. She wielded her stern
qualities like a club. She was always a solid pillar
in whatever group she belonged to. Many a person,
crossing her in some way, had been heard to
compare her to an articulated lorry. She inspired,
on the whole, impregnable images.

CHAPTER 10

In the most unlikely way, on a journey whose theme she privately despised, she was struck by a kind of nemesis. She was the victim of an emotion that, had she detected it in another, would have drawn from her nothing but sarcasm.

The fact is that when she stumbled, disorientated by the journey, into the hotel with her heavy luggage, and found herself being assisted by a jovial middle-aged man with a smoky moustache, she was taken by surprise.

He held her hand and seemed to know that she needed firm steadying. When he lifted her four pieces of luggage as if they were weightless and carried them the full length of the foyer, she was impressed.

With a roguish smile, he said:

'I fix you a vintage Swiss brandy to bring back the beauty to your cheeks.'

When he fixed her with cheerful eyes behind his tortoiseshell glasses, isolating her from all else in the universe, like a connoisseur picking out a pearl from a trunk full of vulgarities, she felt again her forgotten girlishness.

Suddenly she didn't know what to do with her hands, her flaming cheeks, her eyes. Her feet seemed all mixed up. She scurried from the foyer, her neck reddening.

Out in the dark she fumbled among other people's luggage. She got in the way and did not hear a word anyone said. Peculiar music rang in her ears and new sensations darted in her belly. She felt as if something in her might rupture. In a bit of a panic, she leapt to the conclusion that something was wrong with her. With a great effort she managed to bring her emotions under some control.

CHAPTER 11

She saw Sam and Lao talking near the pile of luggage. When she approached they turned to her and smiled. There was something odd about their smiles. Were they smirking? She detected smirks on a few other faces, anyone who just happened to look at her. All men.

Then it occurred to her that someone was playing a trick on her. She couldn't see what the trick was, but she sensed it was there somewhere and they were all in on it. Someone was making a fool of her; she was being set up for a humiliation. Then it crossed her mind that it wasn't a trick. That it was something worse. Someone had put her under a spell.

Beneath Jute's imposing façade lurked a superstitious nature. Superstitious people are susceptible people. Stories rang in her mind of men who had cast spells on women and reduced them to love-slaves. She had heard that love potions could be bought in Egypt and Spain, from Gypsies and Africans and fairground herbalists. She had heard of women who had been used and dumped. They became wandering wrecks, forever pining for the men who had bewitched them, prepared to do anything to get them back.

CHAPTER 12

When she seriously considered that she might be under some kind of spell, the name Malasso flashed into her mind and she woke with a shock. She was at the edge of the lake, staring at the darkness that was the mountain.

She shook her head, not understanding how she had come to be at the lake's edge. She found herself fascinated by the lake and she stared at its glimmering surface, into its depths. Tears were streaming down her face, but she was unaware of them. Then she heard voices. At first she thought they came from the lake.

'Jute isn't herself.'

'She's just staring into space.'

'Maybe Nature's got to her at last.'

'I always wondered what it would take.'

'It's either the lake or it's love.'

'It's the lake. It's having the same effect on me. I want to drown in it and be made new.'

'I think it's love.'

Then they laughed, in irony or jest it was hard to say.

Furious at the merest hint of sentimentality, Jute pulled herself together. As she went back to the hotel, she noticed Propr and Sam a short distance away in the gloaming. They had not noticed her. Tiptoeing back to the hotel, she was determined that she would not fall under the spell of the charming hotelkeeper.

The thing to do, she decided, was not to look at him. This proved difficult; after all it was her job to make sure everyone was checked in properly so she had to talk to him. She tried to be abrupt with him, but could not help thinking him attractive. She tried crushing him with her laconic drawl, bringing the full force of her stern personality down on his head, but he was unperturbed. Rather he seemed enamoured of her brusque manner and became more tender than ever. Instead of destroying the spell, she fell more deeply into it. Fortunately her severe glasses kept her emotions concealed. She checked everyone in, handed around the room keys, and went upstairs.

CHAPTER 13

She was delighted to find that Hans had given her a very splendid room with a large balcony overlooking the lake. The room, with its king-size bed and plush sofas and its sparkling bathroom, at once comfortable and luxurious, softened her spirit.

The twinkling lights across the lake, climbing high up towards the dark sky, drew her to the balcony. She stared at the shadow of the mountain. She breathed deeply. The distant bells sounding over the wind-sculpted surface of the lake made her heart tinkle.

Memories welled up in her, memories of a sad childhood spent among fairy tales and dreams of escape. She dimly remembered that once in her life, when the world was very unclear, a little green being had befriended her. The memory surprised her and she wasn't sure if it had really happened or if she had imagined it. While she was thinking about that, a moment came to her from far away in her past, so far away it seemed to belong to someone else.

She remembered how one evening an angel had

flown out of a book she was reading and she had run to tell her mother about it. She had been answered with such scorn and harshness that the little angel flew out of the window and disappeared forever. After that, Jute never saw anything unusual or wonderful again in the world.

That was the end of her belief in the magical. She grew up to think novels, poems, plays and all art and anything of the imagination a waste of time. She only believed in hard work.

CHAPTER 14

The memory of the departing angel came back to her fleetingly. She leant against the railing and stared at the dance of lights on the lake, and she cried.

Cool breezes played on her face. When she lifted up her eyes to the dark mountain a shadow seemed to pass through her. Everything clouded over for a moment and a stab of panic went through her heart. Suddenly she wanted to climb over the balcony railing and fall into the lake. The desire to drown came on her from nowhere. She was staring at the lake in a honey-dark happiness, when she heard a voice.

'Die while you're happy. It's all downhill from here. Jump!'

The voice was soothing. The beauty of the night almost overcame her, the sublimity of the lake and the mountain, the thousand and one lights that festooned the dark.

'Jump!' the voice coaxed.

For a moment she glimpsed the tranquillity of oblivion.

'Death is beautiful,' the lovely voice whispered.

'It's what you have been longing for all your life. Die while you're young. It's easy. Jump!'

It was easy. She could see herself leaping over. She could feel the rush of the wind. She would leap like a dancer. She would die in the dark loveliness of lake and sky. She would seize the best opportunity in her life for that rarest of blessings, a happy death. She felt the coldness of the railings as she began to climb, but a sudden wind with the fragrance of roses blew in her face. With an effort of will she stumbled back from the edge.

CHAPTER 15

Half expecting to see someone standing behind her, whispering into her ear, she spun around. She was alone. But she had a dim suspicion that Malasso was there in the night.

'What's happening to me?' she wondered aloud.

This softening of her iron façade, this flirtation with love and death, it all filled her with a sweet confusion. She had no idea what she was becoming.

She went back into the room and began to unpack. She looked at her clothes as if she had never seen them before. Then, swaying on uneven ground, she went to the bathroom and took a shower. Feeling a little better, she dressed and went downstairs for dinner. Apart from a few interjections, made purely to keep up form, she had been silent. No one noticed that the alchemy of the journey had already started working on her.

CHAPTER 16

Riley was a creature of changing moods that she could not control. It was the secret of her expressiveness: the plaintive look of a doe and the liveliness of a mime-artist. With sweet sad eyes she was like an orphan with a gift for happiness.

She was skittery and boyish. Her willingness to perform whatever task she was given made her an ideal camera assistant.

She was quite indefinable. When Riley stood still she had the uncanny knack of vanishing. She would simply melt, unnoticed, into a silent space, right before the eye.

Sam often had great difficulty finding her when she was right in front of him. It was a sort of trick she had. She would look straight at you and then she'd disappear. You'd be looking for her and then she would be right there again, like a magician's conjuration.

She had a beguiling way of pulling at the heart, the cunning of a young fox, the swiftness of a desert snake, and the resilience of a whip.

Sam found her intriguing; he had never known anything like her before. Both her parents were alive and well, and yet she seemed like an orphan. She had a handsome boyfriend, and yet she was boyish. When she wore a sexy skirt and make-up she transformed into a head-turning beauty. She obeyed instructions without questions, and yet she had the air of an anarchist.

With an engaging smile that inspired confidence, she went about her mysterious activities, never offering any explanation of herself. She seemed to invent new tricks every day, as if she were not quite made of flesh but of some quicksilver element, some protean substance. More spirit than matter, she seemed a halfway Ariel trapped in a tough and fragile body.

Her facial neutrality was particularly disconcerting. It meant she could be in people's company all day long and they didn't notice. When they thought back on that day they would be struck by an odd note, the sense of a watchful presence which the memory could not quite resolve.

She made holes in time. She made a virtue of her absence, made absence into a kind of force. With her neutrality she turned the dramatic power of the mask into an enigmatic emptiness.

Sam found he had to rediscover Riley all the time. She was like an unfinished painting, alive with potential. Like a chameleon, she was attuned to every mood. And yet she had the strange ability to anticipate a person's next move, sometimes miming it moments before.

No one was in more perfect resonance with Malasso than Riley.

CHAPTER 17

Sam's first encounter with Riley remained an unsolved puzzle. But it was the puzzle that got her hired.

She was the fifth person to answer Sam's advert for a camera assistant. She left a message on Sam's answer machine. It said:

'I'm Riley, your camera assistant, I think. Am I the fifth? I'll be wearing red. Goodbye. Oh, one more thing. I'm worried about my goldfish. Do you like goldfish?'

On the day of the interview, in Sam's flat, only four people showed up. No one was wearing red. The four applicants, two men and two women, were eager and sold themselves well. After the interview, Sam thought any one of them would do. But he was vaguely restless.

He kept expecting the fifth person. He kept going to the door, checking his messages, looking out of the window. He felt twitchy and expectant. A little exasperated, he decided to go for a walk.

In the hallway he saw a boy sitting cross-legged in front of the lift. In his hands was a polystyrene bag in which a languid goldfish swam. The boy gazed at the iridescent goldfish with rapt attention and a half-formed smile. The boy seemed to find something both wonderful and humorous in the whirligig motions of the small fish.

As Sam got closer, the boy stood up. The lift door opened and the boy went in ahead of Sam, but when Sam stepped in he found the lift empty. Thinking that he was hallucinating, he stepped back out and looked around. No one was there. He noticed an empty sweet wrapper on the floor. There were no doors nearby, and the emergency exit was across the hall. It would have taken unnatural swiftness to get there so quickly.

Mystified, Sam went back into the lift. He pressed the button for the ground floor but the lift went up to the fifth instead. When the door opened, Sam had a sudden rush of vertigo. The same boy was sitting cross-legged in front of the lift. He was without the goldfish, wore red trousers, and was apparently asleep.

Before Sam could rouse himself from his stupor the door shut. In the crack he could have sworn he saw the boy run off. The lift cranked without further incident to the ground floor.

CHAPTER 18

It was a bright and beautiful day in Stoke Newington. There were hints of gold in the sky. Sam went for a turn round the green but strayed to a nearby street market. He wished he had brought a camera for it was a rare summery London day and full of signs.

He noticed on a toy stall a white car with the word Arcadia in red letters. He went towards the stall. Then he found himself in front of another that sold goldfish. He watched them circulating in their bubbling aquarium. He was about to turn away when he heard an aerial voice.

'Do you like goldfish then?'

Sam started, looked around, and found no one. People were browsing or wandering past with their shopping. The stall attendant, a bluff red-faced clean-shaven man, was staring at a girl across the street who was bending over to tie her shoelaces. Something made Sam's heart quicken.

'I bought three more to keep Lassie company.'

And there he, or rather she, was. Right in front of him like a mirage made flesh.

'Aren't you . . .?' Sam began, but he never

finished what he was saying for she was gone. Sam turned round, and found her behind him, zipping up her rucksack.

Before Sam could speak again, she said, 'If you want a camera assistant, I'm your fox. I come from the Black Forest in Germany but I live in London. What do you think? Do you like me?'

She was twitching slightly as she spoke.

A little bewitched, he hired her on the spot.

When Sam told Jim about having hired the girl, he kept quiet about her strangeness. She would be his secret weapon, his mascot during the vicissitudes of the filming. She turned out to be more than a mascot. She was a hard-working, efficient machine of an assistant, a faithful hound with a mercurial quality who contrived often to be unseen.

CHAPTER 19

When they arrived at the hotel in the town of B—, something changed in Riley that made her more visible than she had been. People who hadn't noticed her previously suddenly asked her questions. Lao found that if he stared vacantly into the space where she sat he could fix her in the flesh, make her palpable.

Riley felt this subtle change in herself and it made her uneasy, which made her fidget. She took to sliding away from people's glances, hiding when she sensed eyes settling on her. But her attempts at hiding, at sliding away, only made her more noticeable.

'What the hell is wrong with you?' Jim had asked her suddenly at dinner that night.

'I don't know,' was all Riley could say. 'Something's in the air. It's as if someone I know but can't see is here . . . My skin feels like it's on fire.'

Jim no longer saw her for she had become still while she spoke, and when she was still it was often difficult to see her.

Besides, Jim had already returned to his exposition of the will.

CHAPTER 20

Apart from the occasional comment which she made without wanting to, Riley stayed silent for the rest of the dinner.

No one noticed when she slipped away. She went out into the dark and sat on a bench at the edge of the lake, listening to the barely audible whisperings of waves on the shore. She felt the presence of the one whom she could not see, while the mountain wind soothed for a time the heat on her skin.

CHAPTER 21

That night Propr lay in bed and listened to the fragments of sound from the beginning of time.

He listened to the mountain, the wind, and the lapping of water on the rim of the earth. He listened to the lake, heard its songs. He heard the dance of water and rock, and the winds twisting round the crags of the mountain.

Slightly drunk, he took soundings from the new place he was in. From the sounds he heard he gave the world form. Sounds created worlds for him, worlds more interesting than worlds seen. For Propr, hearing was believing, hearing was being. Seeing things reduced them for him, stripped them of mystery.

As he lay there, absolutely still, he could hear wind-chimes in a distant village. He could hear the wind slapping the rugged face of rock on the other side of the lake.

CHAPTER 22

His listening led him into childhood moments: the arc of a swing, the silence between tocks of a grandfather clock, a heron taking flight across a meadow.

He remembered the piping of birds on hot afternoons in the hills, the river murmuring along the stony banks, insects in the summer stillness, the whirring of a quail's wings in the Welsh woodlands.

Propr dissolved into listening as other people dissolved into their fantasies. It was the closest he ever got to a religious experience. While others would go to church to worship, Propr would sit on the banks of a river, or lie on the floor of a forest, and lose himself in concerts of sound.

He would listen with eyes closed to the most remote of sounds: the fall of a feather, the distant dance of a bumble bee, waves on the riverbank, the wind in faraway trees, the murmur of the open sky, even the diaphanous light of the sun.

Listening to such subtleties, he could no longer distinguish between earth and sky, water and wind. All merged into a listening that opened out into the infinite vastness of being.

CHAPTER 23

In his hotel room he listened himself into an expansive world, like a universe glimpsed at sunset, in an aeroplane high above the clouds.

He listened to the spaces. He heard the mountain as a cascade of dark eternal melodies. He heard a magic being riding the surface of the lake. She was the woman of his dreams, and she faded into the wind.

He was happy in his listening till he heard them making love a few rooms away. His mood darkened. Then he heard it again, the sinister whispering that had haunted him ever since the journey to Arcadia began.

Endlessly repeated, like a child's taunt in the playground of Hades:

Find the treasure . . . Find the treasure . . . Find the treasure . . .

BOOK VI

ELYSIAN STONES

SECTION I

CHAPTER 1

Sunlight streamed through the stained-glass window of their awakening. They rose like dolphins from the blue depths of sleep. New eyes opened on the hotel room, taking in the shining wooden floor, the white ceiling, and the Giorgione print on the lilac wall.

Their consciousness had been cleansed in sleep. Everything was made new. They felt a thrill and a freshness in every fibre. It was as if, until that morning, they had never lived before.

Sunlight made all the colours brilliant. They were struck dumb by the wonderful light of the lake and the white summits of the mountain.

CHAPTER 2

How does one awaken to the quintessence of such a day?

How does one live it right, drink in its magic without the little flaws in one's temperament spoiling the promised beauties of being?

They felt happiness pouring in through the windows, pouring its golden rays into their core. It was the kind of day that makes the body, like Faust, utter the vertiginous cry:

Make this moment my eternity.

CHAPTER 3

Rising up into such a dawn, Lao and Mistletoe felt like Adam and Eve in an alternative Genesis. They did not eat of the apple. They had not been cast out to wander, as Adam and Eve had, for millennia in what Jacob Böhme called *the fury and wrath of nature*.

They woke with a sense of grace and good fortune. History was the nightmare, and joy the true reality. They went about on tiptoes, barely speaking, so as not to breathe evil on such a blessed day. They went through their morning rituals, gathering flowers in their hearts.

It was Lao's day off and the rest of the crew had gone filming. Lao and Mistletoe had the day's discoveries all to themselves.

Dawn was the garden redeemed by sleep.

CHAPTER 4

They watched a steamboat sail past their hotel, blasting its horn. They went down to the lake, whose water now was gold and blue.

The air was crisp and clean. It made them breathe consciously. They drew the ionised air of lake and mountain deep into their bellies. Then they exhaled, emptying their lungs.

Breathing deeply cleared their minds and prepared them for the unusual. They were like children on the first day of their holiday who have woken early and gone to the garden to play.

They breathed to the rhythm of their walking, cleaning out the years of neglect. One's breathing is shallow in cities, thought Lao. Shallow breath, shallow life: as you breathe, so you live. He felt taller for the intake of mountain air.

The quality of the light by the lake seemed to transfigure Mistletoe. It became her element. She walked on light, gazing at the mountains without seeing them.

They took their shoes off and walked barefoot on the smooth grass. They walked by the side of the lake and let the dew and the light work on them.

CHAPTER 5

There are things whose beauty grows the more attention you give them, Mistletoe was thinking. They admired the whimsical houses of the town. Lao noticed a church; it was small and beautiful. Something about the dawn made it seem like a sign.

They crossed the road, went over to the church and were disappointed to find its door locked. It occurred to them that they were meant to receive their message from a less obvious door. They went round to the back, and came upon the dead.

The graves were neatly laid out. There were gravestones and steles of great beauty and variety. There were marble and granite gravestones, inscribed with names and dates of birth and death, along with a biblical quotation or a note of lamentation. The gravestones had Greek, looped, or Maltese crosses, exquisitely masoned. The paths between were bordered with roses, lilies, fuchsias, and carnations. There were even orchids. The sense of order was astonishing.

Death had been made into a thing of splendour. There were glazed pictures of the dead on every grave. The images in living colours were spooky in their realism. There were fresh flowers in a vase in front of each stone. The dead were being kept alive every day in thought, the ancient as well as the newly dead.

Some gravestones spoke of the deaths of babies, of children, young men at war, old men at sea, young ladies snatched away too soon. One woman died *for love*; another died *for peace*. Most died of time. On some gravestones there were marble busts of the departed. Most of the graves had lamps that burned perpetually.

It was the most enchanting cemetery they had ever seen, a communal work of memory. Its labyrinthine paths led to innumerable forms of grieving. It was grieving as an art.

CHAPTER 6

Lao and Mistletoe wandered through this strange cemetery where the dead seemed luckier than the living. It made death seem a happy place.

Then they noticed some women in black in tears around a grave. They gazed in silence at a photograph on an unfinished gravestone.

It was time to leave. They didn't want to be tourists at other people's grief. Both of their parents were still alive, and they didn't know what grief was yet. They were in a happy dream, and didn't know it.

Watching the women's tears they felt, from a distance, the chill shadow of loss. They felt like children in the forecourt of death.

Dark thoughts had entered the radiant day.

CHAPTER 7

They left the cemetery, crossed the road again, and walked on in silence. The cemetery had altered them.

For the first time, Mistletoe really saw the mountains. When she did, so did Lao. As if they had been given surprise gifts, they exclaimed at the same time.

With death-cleansed eyes, Mistletoe saw the blue mountain range, the jagged high rocks, and the smoky peaks. The rock-faces were of ice and stone, defined by a sky of uncanny blue. Thick white light poured out from the dense clouds around the mountaintop.

She saw how the mountain shaded into smoky blue distances, like matter dissolving into spirit, or spirit condensing into matter. Emotions choked her and suddenly she had an attack of homesickness, but it was for a home mysterious to her, connected to the remote mountain peaks fading into those invisible distances. She steadied herself on Lao's shoulder for a moment.

CHAPTER 8

'This town is merging with its dead,' said Lao suddenly, after they had resumed walking.

Then he was silent. His words stirred many thoughts in her. She knew enough to let the silence enrich the words. Working with silence was an art they were constantly refining.

'I get the feeling it yields its mysteries when you encounter the spirit of its dead,' Lao said after a while.

It was Mistletoe's turn to be silent. Walking on the dew in the grass, they breathed as much through the soles of their feet as through their noses.

Lao gazed into the distance where rock was indistinguishable from air.

'On the mountains towns like this are disappearing into legend,' he said.

'It treats its dead so beautifully, like newborn children,' said Mistletoe.

'The silence here mirrors the silence there, among peaks of snow.'

They walked on. After a long moment Mistletoe drew in her breath.

'What?'

'We have just passed into the mirror of the town. There's a touch of silver in my eyes,' said Mistletoe.

They both laughed. They felt unaccountably inspired.

'Like incense, flowers with their beauty bear our thoughts faster to other realms,' said Lao.

'The dead hear what we are thinking about them as clearly as we hear the wind streaming down the mountains,' said Mistletoe.

'Somewhere in us the absent is most present.'

'It takes as much effort to keep the dead alive in us as to keep the living present to us.'

They were approaching a pier. Beyond it was the sparkling lake and the cloud-crowned mountain.

CHAPTER 9

'What can you do with all this beauty? The frosted peaks, the silver lake, the light, this dawn?' Lao asked. 'It fills my heart, I want to do something with it, and I don't know what.'

'I know,' Mistletoe said. 'It's a kind of despair. Beauty makes me despair sometimes.'

'Beauty often makes me think of death.'

'Can you be so happy that you want to die?'

'Is there a link?'

'Some people say death is the greatest happiness, that it's not the dead we really mourn, but ourselves who are still here.'

They gazed at the lake.

'It's the best kept secret.'

'If we knew how beautiful death was, we wouldn't fear it.'

'We would have more courage.'

'To live our lives.'

They both fell silent, but went on walking, their breathing slower and deeper. Then Mistletoe broke the silence.

'I think death must hold the key to life.'

204

'Or maybe life holds the secret of death.'

'Perhaps they need each other – like light and darkness.'

'But which is light, and which is darkness?'

'Life is darkness.'

'So death is light.'

'Yes, we're living in darkness.'

'And we'll die in the light.'

'We have to find light in darkness . . .'

'And begin again.'

'Rising and falling.'

'Till we get to the mountaintop.'

'But we need some lunch before that.'

'And wine.'

'And a siesta.'

'And some reading.'

'And some kissing.'

They laughed and wandered on up the jetty. They mingled for a few moments among the tourists who were waiting to board the steamboat that would take them to the villages further down the lake.

They walked on through the streets, staring at the cottages, the gabled houses, the fairy-tale chalets.

They hadn't gone long when, on looking back, they noticed that the church was further away than they thought it would be, as if it had moved.

They went on a little longer, and then they thought they should make their way home to the hotel in time for lunch. But when they turned back everything seemed different. They were lost.

CHAPTER 10

The air had become murky though there were no clouds in the sky. They heard raucous noises up ahead, people talking loudly and all at once. An orchestra sounded jarring notes close by. There were vintage cars parked along the road. Lao and Mistletoe were bewildered.

They came to a white open-topped car with a bunch of violets visible on the front seat and a card with words scribbled on it which they didn't have time to decipher because they suddenly noticed someone standing next to them. A tall well-dressed gentleman in a morning suit and a grey top hat with the air of a successful banker stood there. He had just sunk his teeth into a split pomegranate when they asked him the way back to the hotel. To their surprise he threw his head back and laughed. It was very disconcerting. They could see the red seeds in his open mouth. As he laughed they had a chance to look at the card.

Greater authority
Hath Christ

Who rose from death
Than Christ
Before his death.

CHAPTER 11

Lao and Mistletoe exchanged glances. Thinking that the man had not heard their question, they asked it again. He stopped laughing and regarded them with pity.

'There's no way you'll get a hotel in this town, dear boy,' he said, taking another bite from his half-eaten pomegranate. 'It's all full up. It's been full up all season.'

He must have noticed the strange look on their faces for, in a more genial tone, he said:

'Everybody is here, you know. The rich, the famous, the fatuous, dear lady, are all here. Film stars, shipping magnates, great beauties, American tycoons, and the thousands that go where they go, are all here. There's not a single room to be had, for God or money.'

The look of consternation on their faces deepened. The man smiled ruefully.

'As you can see, I'm leaving. I've had enough. I'm finished.'

He pulled out a black handkerchief and wiped his face. He became solemn.

'The town is ruined,' he said sadly. 'Ruined by

the rich and famous. It's over-run and over-exposed. That's the price of fame, dear boy, the deadly price of fame.'

Lao and Mistletoe looked at one another.

'I know what you're thinking,' the man said, looking at them with a thoughtful smile. 'But it's true. First the rich, then the rest. After that, hysteria.' He fixed them each with a piercing stare. 'Do you know what we have done?'

Lao and Mistletoe shook their heads.

'We have sucked the place dry,' he said. 'We have torn up its flowers, fornicated in its cemetery, and revelled in its churches. We have sucked its teats dry. We have spread debauchery everywhere. That's what we do.'

He gave them a mournful look.

'Then we move on, find another town by a lake or the sea, somewhere unspoilt, and we do it all over again. We make a place famous, and then we ruin it. But I'm leaving, I'm finished.'

The last bit of pomegranate disappeared into his mouth. He gave them an avuncular smile.

'Good luck to you both. I hope you find somewhere to stay in the encroaching darkness. You look so innocent. Lambs to the slaughter. But beware the wine of fame, its intoxication, its madness.'

Then he raised his hat to them, slid into the white car, and sped off, mirage into a mirage, without raising dust.

CHAPTER 12

Not knowing what to make of the man's utterances, they went on walking through the unfamiliar streets till they came to their hotel. They were puzzled to find a scene of drunken rowdiness in its forecourt. The building looked bright as if freshly painted. It had a bustling air and a large signboard over the entrance which wasn't there before. Spilling out of the doorway, noisy in the garden, were men in morning suits and women in slinky silk dresses and demure hats. They were all talking at once and were drunk and jolly. A man with a waxed moustache and a fluted glass of champagne in one hand caught sight of Lao and Mistletoe and pointed at them and said something to his companions. They turned and stared as though they had never seen anything like them in the world.

'We'd better go,' Lao said. 'I think we're in the wrong time.'

They turned and hurried back in the direction they had come, trying to control their panic.

CHAPTER 13

They half walked, half ran, till they were in sight of the pier. They took off their sandals and walked on the cool grass. They saw the little church again and crossed the road to wander among the beautiful gravestones of marble, granite and alabaster. They walked on the straight paths and looked at the carnations and violets and at the busts and pictures of the dead. They paid attention to the dates on the gravestones.

In the cemetery they calmed down a bit. The lighted lamps and flowers and the Elysian beauty of the place instilled in them some tranquillity.

They began touching the stones, and noticed a tingling in their fingertips. It was Mistletoe who saw the photograph first, the glazed picture of a man. The inscription read:

Tom Woolnoth
Investment Banker
Died in a Car Accident
Departed in a Hurry
1888–1928

When they saw the picture the air settled, their heads cleared, and the magic quality of the light returned.

CHAPTER 14

The mountain shone like crystals and the lake shimmered.

Freed of an oppressive weight in their heads, they looked at the pictures on the graves with new respect.

Sending out a silent blessing to all the dead, they left the cemetery, crossed the road and walked barefoot on the grass, and breathed gently.

They did not allude to their experience, choosing to pretend that nothing odd had happened, that they had merely passed through fragments of a dream floating in the air.

They kept their eyes firmly fixed on the mountain, till they got to their hotel. They lunched on salad and grilled fish and a glass of Sancerre, and went upstairs to sleep off their perplexity.

SECTION II

CHAPTER 1

Lao woke up screaming. He had been muttering incoherent words in his sleep, kicking and clutching at the air.

Mistletoe was already awake. She had been sketching the mountain. When he woke from his nightmare, she regarded him coolly. He got up and looked around the room as though to reassure himself of his surroundings. He gazed at the lake. Then he picked up his copy of Goethe's *Faust Part Two*, and began reading.

Now that he was up, Mistletoe went to the balcony to get a fuller view of the mountain. Breathing evenly, she disappeared into the mountain she was sketching. She vanished into its monumental form and the ravishing beauty of the view. She became pure being lost in pure beauty.

Lao meanwhile was making a complicated journey into the book. They were now at the Imperial Palace, in Germany. Economic problems threatened the state; and Mephistopheles had invented paper money, anticipating future reality.

The Emperor expressed the desire to see Helen of Troy; and Faust charged Mephistopheles to make this come true.

CHAPTER 2

While reading, Lao travelled back to the ancient world. Faust was now in a coma, and they travel in his consciousness to the great underworld, a combination of Egypt and Greece where sirens dwell side by side with the Sphinx, griffins with wise centaurs and Nereids, and ants speaking in splendid verse. All beings that have had an imaginative existence live here in this underworld, deep in the consciousness of the human race. The gods are real. It is to this world they go to find Helen of Troy, the great beauty of legend.

As their guide on this quest, they have a homunculus. Made in a test tube, a creature of science, the homunculus wants above all things to be a man. He needs the magic stuff of humanity. It is his very incompleteness that makes him a perfect guide into the depths of the human psyche.

CHAPTER 3

Lao struggled with the book, in just the same way he struggled in his dream. And the book was a strange dream indeed, one of the strangest ever composed. Lao was confused by it, but determined to understand.

He knew he wasn't alone in his confusion. Many have thought Goethe's *Faust Part Two* incomprehensible. He knew that even the great French poet Gérard de Nerval, its first French translator, deplored its obscurity. But Lao was fascinated by its boldness and wildness, and how it belonged constantly to the future.

To read the book is to journey into the mind of Faust, the representative mind. It was in the underworld of that mind that they sought the ideal that is Helen of Troy.

CHAPTER 4

Why was Lao making this journey? Because he suspected that on the journey might be found the keys to the treasure house of Arcadia.

So far they had been travelling in the world, by train. But to find the essence of Arcadia he would have to travel in a different way, into a text, into himself, to its original and lasting place. He would enter Arcadia through the collective unconscious. This Arcadia would not be found on the map. Helen of Troy is the key to that realm.

CHAPTER 5

Lao lost himself in Goethe's verse, the peculiar characters, the complex philosophies. His mind cleared only when he looked up and saw Mistletoe's outline against the mountain. She sat still, lost in the rugged mountain of her ancestry.

All things are ideas, he thought. Solid things are condensations of primal energy. That is why mountains near lakes enchant us. They suggest different stages of the creative process. Things we touch and feel reassure us. That's why material things are comforting. They make the body feel at home. But something in the body must also feel at home in the body. It is that something inside us that responds to beauty.

The mountains move me because they touch something in me older than time. It is to the beauty in me that the beauty of the lake and sky speaks. The body, alive, breathes air. The spirit breathes light.

CHAPTER 6

Inspired, he went into a deeper meditation. Arcadia, he thought, is an idea. It began inside us. But abstractions defeat us. We need real and visible things. Even miracles must be concrete. To believe in the existence of God we need God to put in an appearance, to be visible, which would make us believe less. We lose our way because we can only believe in evidence. We lose our way with the very senses we use to verify.

Seeing is believing, they say. But what is seeing? Do we see with the eyes only? Do we not only see the effects of light? The eyes are imprecise instruments of complete vision, he thought. We need higher instruments. The instrument of poetry, the organ of intuition, which could supply to consciousness the highest data.

CHAPTER 7

While he was reflecting, he attempted a definition of Arcadia.

A resting place between journeys.
Flowers in a garden.
Trees among rocks.
A beautiful little town along a highway.
An oasis.
A weekend among week days.
Poetry in the midst of prose.
A drawing among words.
A song on a journey.
Music in the silence.
Silence in the music.
An act of love in the midst of hatred.
A dialectical pause.
Holidays.

He let his mind soar. He remembered that Novalis somewhere had written that philosophy is homesickness. So is beauty, he thought. But homesickness for where, or what? For a home that no home on earth can satisfy, a home of which Arcadia is a symbol. A balm for that perennial homesickness. The promise of complete happiness, deferred.

SECTION III

CHAPTER 1

In the late afternoon, they went exploring again. This time they ventured beyond the bridge. Mistletoe led the way, following an unerring instinct. They crossed a patch of wasteland and went under a flyover. Suddenly they heard music and went towards it, walking along a path and climbing a hill till they saw a wood.

They had come upon a music festival in a clearing in the wood. A crowd of people were jumping up and down and singing along to a rock anthem pounding from a stage. There were caravans and portable lavatories on the edges of the clearing, and stalls selling hamburgers, hot-dogs, roasted chicken, beers, soft drinks, popcorn, T-shirts, books, CDs, multicoloured scarves, magic rings, and necklaces. There was even a Tarot card stall. Here at last were the young people of the town.

Lao and Mistletoe were relieved. They had begun to suspect the town of having no young people, as if some spirit of negation had driven them all away.

Coming upon a festival in the woods was exciting, as if they had wandered into a legend.

They mingled with the young men in hats, the young women in pretty dresses, and didn't think of themselves as outsiders. They bought soft drinks and hot-dogs and watched the peculiar dances.

But Lao and Mistletoe did attract attention because they were different. People clustered round them, wanting to talk to them, but didn't have the courage.

Mistletoe began dancing. She danced on one spot, moving her hips, shaking her shoulders. It was a controlled dance. Lao brooded. He was watchful, his expression impenetrable.

They both thought the music very bad, but they listened. Then Lao growled out something which Mistletoe didn't hear. But she grasped its intention. She said:

'Why did you wake up screaming?'

'Why did you stare at me coldly?'

'You destroyed my mood.'

'What mood?'

'I was trying to draw the cloud over the mountain, to capture something quite difficult.'

'And so?'

'I was just discovering something and then you screamed, and frightened it away.'

'How was I to know that? I was asleep.'

'How was I to protect myself from your nightmare?'

'I can't say I'm sorry.'

'Of course you can't; you're a monster.'

'Monsters don't have nightmares. They are nightmares.'

'What about gods? Do they have nightmares?'

'Some people would say this world is the bad dream of a god.'

'We are all gods,' said Mistletoe.

'Gods of mud.'

'Okay, we're not gods. We only contain gods.'

'You got that from a sacred Indian book.'

'Yes.'

'"All the gods are within us, like cows in a cowshed."'

'Well remembered. Anyway, why did you scream?'

'I thought I had diverted you from that question.'

'I know some of your tricks. I know the things you want to tell me.'

'How?'

'Oh, how, how, how. They are usually the questions you don't answer, the ones you deflect.'

'Really?'

'You're not a piece of music, you know. You're not to be got, any more than I am. When we're in tune, it's lovely; when we're not, it's frustrating. You ask me how I know when you want to really tell me something. Pure instinct, that's all.'

'What are you talking about?'

'Forget it.'

'I think I lost you there. Do you want a drink?'

'I'm drunk.'

'Already?'

'I was drunk when we left the hotel.'

'From what?'

'From drawing the mountains. It did something weird to my head. I'm a little giddy.'

'You've been soaring, my dear.'

'My head's been expanding.'

'Now you're big-headed.'

'Not nearly as much as you are. So, tell me why you screamed.'

'Do you really want to know?'

'Of course not.'

'Then I'll tell you.'

'Even if I don't want to hear?'

'Absolutely.'

'Then I won't listen.'

'Excellent.'

'I'm not listening, but carry on.'

'I had this dream,' said Lao. 'In the dream Malasso was showing me a map of the world. I looked at it, and fell in. I fell into the world. I fell and fell till I landed at the precise point in the map that I was standing on to begin with. Malasso laughed and said: *This is the Arcadia you're looking for.* I didn't understand what he meant.'

Lao paused. The music from the band had got louder, and the shouting and singing along amplified it. They moved further away.

'In the same dream Malasso showed me another map. It was a map of the universe, vast and three-dimensional. I got lost in it. Centuries went by. I woke up in this place where there was a lake and a mountain. You were on the mountaintop dancing naked with the circus folk. I called to you, and you turned, saw me, and screamed. Then the circus folk, like murderous bacchantes, came at me. I ran and suddenly found myself with Malasso. He showed me the map again. Then he said: *This is what will happen when you find the treasure . . .* I still didn't understand.'

Looking around, Lao saw that the crowds were denser. The musicians were performing another song, a ballad, and it was not as loud as the previous one.

'And then in the same dream he showed me a third map.'

'Is this still Malasso?'

'Yes. The third map was tiny. It was minuscule. It was microscopic. I peered into it, and saw everything: the first map, the second map, my life, your life, the whole earth, all dreams, all fishes, angels, cloud formations, fourth dimensional beings. As I gazed I fell into this map, and I wandered the world, looking for someone I knew. I discovered that I knew everyone. All things were familiar to me. It was disconcerting.'

Lao paused again and shook his head as if to rid himself of an unpleasant sensation. Mistletoe listened with a neutral expression.

'Then I came to a gravestone. It had one word inscribed on it in gold letters: ARCADIA. As I stared at the word there was a mighty noise. The earth cleaved apart and the tomb opened and a man stepped out. He had a strange glow. There was something about him, something frightening. Then I realised what it was.'

Lao stopped.

'What was it?'

'It was his tranquillity,' said Lao in such a soft voice that she almost missed it. 'But that's not it. The really weird thing is I noticed that he was me.'

'You?'

'Yes, me. A better, wiser, transfigured me, shining with the tranquil authority of truth.'

Lao's face turned grim.

'Then the really scary thing happened.'

'What?'

'This other me, this transformed me, approached, and I fled. At least I tried to, but couldn't. Then he enfolded me in an electrifying embrace which I could not withstand. It was horrible. It felt as if I was scalded. I screamed, and woke up to your cool stare.'

CHAPTER 2

A warm applause rose from the crowd at the conclusion of the ballad. The performance had ended, and another band took over.

Mistletoe said nothing. She was letting the recounted dream settle. Her response would take a form she didn't know yet. She didn't want to force it. Lao understood this, but he still wanted a word from her. It was always a risk telling a dream, and he didn't want his dream to disappear into silence.

'Do you understand how your cool stare made me feel?'

She looked at him with neutral eyes, and said nothing. She was never good with anything resembling a direct accusation. When it became clear that she was not going to say anything, he shrugged and went off into the crowd. It was a way of regaining something of the integrity lost in speaking of his dream.

Mistletoe stayed where she was, and watched his head vanish into the crowd.

CHAPTER 3

She drew a line on him and intersected it with another, and kept track of his motion through the crowd. How easy it is for two people to lose one another, she thought. She was aware that he had left because of her unresponsiveness, but she couldn't help it.

Mistletoe never failed to be amazed at how Lao used disharmony as a weapon for harmony. If she loved him less this weapon would long ago have destroyed their relationship. He was doing it now, she felt. He was wielding disharmony, threatening the ruination of their cultivated Arcadia. And for what? Because she had not responded to his dream? She knew that was not the reason. The real reason he had gone off was her coldness. Of all the negative qualities, the one he disliked most was coldness. To him coldness was an active disengagement of self, a minus zero emotional condition, an utter absence of love. It was for him the real negation, and she knew this.

If that was the case it would take a while to bring him round. It would take an inspired gesture, a sustained warming of the heart, a re-engaging of the imagination. She secretly enjoyed the challenge of creating harmony between them again, working her way round the perversity of wanting and yet resisting a rapprochement.

CHAPTER 4

While she stood there, in the midst of a dancing crowd, a young man approached her. He was good-looking, in his twenties, and seemed at first glance very sure of himself.

He wore jeans and a T-shirt with a musical logo. His dark hair was long and his eyes blue. On his right arm there was the tattoo of a Tarot card.

He smiled.

'I've been watching you,' he said. 'You're very interesting. Such interesting eyes too . . .'

Oh dear, thought Mistletoe, just what I need. Some good-looking guy talking to me when Lao is in a huff.

Then she mentally closed off the space around her. To the young man she said:

'I'm not on my own, and really I'm not that interesting, but thank you.'

'No, no, no, I'm an expert on interesting people,' he said.

Mistletoe scrutinised him coolly. Round his neck hung a pendant of the ankh, an Egyptian symbol, along with a copper skull, a crooked cross, and a five-pointed star. When she looked closer she saw that the Tarot card on his forearm was that of The Fool. Then she noticed his sad eyes.

'I'm with the band,' he said. 'Do you like our music?'

Mistletoe said nothing and kept her gaze neutral.

'If you like our music, we will be successful. If you don't, we will start again. I trust your eyes.'

'Start again,' said Mistletoe.

'From the beginning?'

'From scratch.'

'What is scratch?'

Mistletoe stared at him. She could not think of the word in German, French, or Italian. A little helplessly, and with more emphasis, she said, 'From scratch.'

'Scratch?'

'From the beginning. Go back to ABC. Dig deep. Start all over. Trust heart, not eyes.'

She began to move away but the young man blocked her path.

'Help me!' he said. 'Help me. I need you. You have something special. I knew it at once. Help me!'

Mistletoe felt her face getting hot. She was bewildered.

'This town is being forgotten,' the young man cried. 'We are vanishing. What can I do? Are we dying? My life is fading every day. I need to be famous. Help me! Teach me what you know . . .'

It occurred to Mistletoe that the young man was under a profound misapprehension, that he thought her someone she wasn't. He was so passionate and full of despair that she didn't know how to disillusion him.

While she was backing off, Mistletoe had a sudden vision. It resolved into an image, and then it was gone. She turned and pushed her way through the crowd. She needed to breathe. She struggled through the jostling dancers. She could not find Lao. She could not breathe.

'Help me!'

Mistletoe was perplexed. She had noticed in the past that when she and Lao had a little break-up, men seemed to find her unusually attractive. It was as if his leaving made her magnetic. It seemed to be happening again.

She couldn't breathe.

The vision she had needed to be shared.

'Help me!'

The tone of the young man's voice, insistent and pleading, finally got to Mistletoe. She turned to him and stared with icy ferocity into the eyes that were seeking something he feared he might never find. Then she pointed to the ground at his feet. She pointed three times, with great authority. The young man fell to his knees and looked up at her expectantly.

'Don't get up,' she said.

'Till when?'

'Till you can save yourself,' she said, turning and pushing through the dancers.

She needed to breathe. She tried to track Lao

in the crowd but had lost his vectors. He wasn't there. Where could he be? She found herself next to the bandstand. She felt the music in her solar plexus. The people around her were dancing as if their bodies were alien to them.

She fled from the stage and went to a nearby drinking tent. But he hadn't been there, she could tell. Where was he? He must be quite angry to have made himself so hard to find. The music got worse. Outside, the crowd thickened. She struggled through, and found herself pressed against the stage again. I shouldn't have been so cold to him, she thought, as the music pounded around her. Why did I have to be cold to him anyway? I couldn't help it. I can't breathe. It just came over me. One moment's coldness and he loves me no more. I need to breathe.

Then she blacked out beside the stage.

'Only among the dead can the treasure be found. Tell him to go there,' someone whispered into her ear.

She breathed suddenly and woke up with a start. Everything cleared. The music was gentler. The crowd had thinned. Lao stood a short distance away, staring at her with a shy smile on his face.

CHAPTER 5

'Here's what I found out . . .' he began.

'You hid from me.'

'This town used to be incredibly famous . . .'

'You're cruel.'

'We've been invited to a party later tonight . . .'

'Where did you go?'

'I went discovering.'

'You left me.'

'You shut me out.'

'I can't seem to stop it when it comes over me.'

'You can – it's your mind, you know.'

'Is it? Sometimes others have access.'

'Only if you let them.'

'I've heard whisperings.'

'What about?'

'Nothing.' She smiled. 'Tell me what you found out.'

'This town used to be really famous. Everyone used to come here. Now it has chosen to be a secret.'

'Why?'

'Because of what success did to it.'

'Is this a good idea?'

'The young don't think so. They think the town is fading away. It bothers them. Should we go to the party tonight?'

'Yes. I could do with a dance.'

'So could I.'

CHAPTER 6

They watched as the festival wound down, the musicians began unplugging their instruments and the crowds dispersed. The grounds were strewn with chicken bones, paper napkins, half-eaten hot-dogs, empty cigarette packets, beer cans.

As the crowd cleared Mistletoe caught a glimpse of the young man still kneeling. Lao saw him too. He was causing a bit of a stir. Lao said quietly, 'Let's get out of here. I smell obsession.'

They went through the woods, over the hill, and passed beneath the flyover. They walked towards the town in silence.

CHAPTER 7

They sat on a bench, near the pier, and stared at the mountains. The moving clouds made the mountains move. The sky made the world unreal.

Boats and steamers and gilded yachts glided past on the lake.

Lao wondered if the world wasn't an analogy for a world not seen.

This is what the mountains and the lake did to him. They made him want to change his life, to become more, to be more alive.

The mountains gave him a sense of things greater than history. They didn't make him feel humble; they made him feel imperfectly developed. They made him ache for an unrealised grandeur.

The power of the mountains encompassed Mistletoe. She surrendered herself to it and shone like the lake.

BOOK VII

AN INTERVAL IN THE ENCHANTMENT OF LIVING

SECTION I

CHAPTER 1

That evening they had a muted dinner with the rest of the crew. Everyone seemed different somehow, and a little preoccupied. Jute, strangely on edge, kept looking at the door, as if expecting someone to walk in. She was wearing a velvet evening dress and looked pretty in her make-up. Riley kept twitching in her seat. Propr hummed a tune to himself through most of dinner. They all drank rather a lot and talked at length about the day's shoot. Sam had achieved his wish. Hanging from the helicopter door with a winch, he had managed splendid and difficult shots of the mountain.

'I have never been more scared in my life,' Husk said about her first helicopter experience.

'How did you overcome your fear?' asked Mistletoe.

'Sheer necessity,' replied Husk.

They talked about the flight, how the winds on the mountains had caused hair-raising moments.

As they were talking, Jim was drinking steadily. He looked haunted. He muttered something about the budget and about money expected which hadn't

251

arrived, but the others were too engrossed in the technicalities of filming trains from helicopters to hear him.

'Are you all right?' Lao asked Jim eventually.

'Why do you ask?'

'You're unusually quiet.'

'I talked too much yesterday. I hope you didn't pay any attention to what I said about you at dinner. I got a little carried away. I'm not quite myself.'

'None of us are. It's something about the journey.'

'Maybe.'

'Did you know that the word devil means the father of lies?'

'So what?'

'So your experience was with the father of lies.'

'Right,' Jim said dully.

'The Devil, it would seem, is the greatest illusion of all.'

'Really . . .'

'In the Tarot, The Devil represents adversity. They say it is the reason why we sometimes run with fire on our heads towards the sea, or towards Arcadia.'

Lao could see that Jim did not want to talk about any of it. His face was closed and turned away. Then as if a new thought had occurred to him, Jim said:

'So you believe, like Goethe, that in some weird way the Devil's doing God's work?'

'I have heard it whispered,' Lao said, surprised

himself by what he was saying, 'that behind the mask of the Devil is an angel's face.'

Jim said nothing.

'Are you all right?' Lao asked again.

Jim looked at him thoughtfully for a long moment. Then he said, 'This journey will either destroy me, or it will be the making of me.'

CHAPTER 2

On that late summer's evening, Lao and Mistletoe crept away from the group and made for the party. The wind was warm. The sky was gold and blue, deepening to indigo. The breath of summer flowers on the wind made them feel good to be alive.

Above the houses, something glowed. It was as if the visible world concealed an enigma whose answer lies in pure dream. As they walked, Lao had the weird sense that the world was a dream, and that behind that dream unknown gods watch humanity. The notion troubled him, made him shiver. But the sense of being watched persisted. Maybe I'm imagining it, he thought. But what if I'm not? Who is watching and why? Is it to see what we do with this magic stuff of life? Then why don't they intervene from time to time, Lao wondered?

Maybe they do, he thought. Maybe it's all a dream in which the dreamer learns. Then we wake to an understanding that we dimly had all along.

CHAPTER 3

They passed gabled houses, wooden chalets, picture-book buildings. The clock on the clock tower impersonated the moon. The streets were empty and the houses silent. The statue of a legendary hero appeared in the dark. The town was like a stage upon which an arcane ritual was to be enacted.

'Do you get the sense we're being watched?' Mistletoe asked.

'I was just thinking that.'

'Maybe we're the ones . . .'

'Doing the watching?'

'Watching ourselves?'

'In a supernatural way.'

'I was just thinking that too.'

It occurred to them then that this feeling might be happiness. They were perfectly balanced between illusion and reality.

CHAPTER 4

If they knew how, they could have walked through the mirror of beauty into a shining world. In that moment, between strides, they could have seen that nothing was meant to be, but only what they made it. They could have rewritten their lives on the margins of the book of life.

It was a near perfect moment for them under the stars.

But the mood of the party would change all that.

CHAPTER 5

The dancehall was dark, smoky, overcrowded. The music was loud. Strobe lights writhed across walls and snaked over dancers. Everyone seemed a little nervous. The women had glassy-eyed stares and the men hung around striking listless poses like people awaiting the messengers of the new.

Then the music improved. Lao and Mistletoe began to dance. They danced to cleanse the body of staleness. They danced themselves into a controlled trance, into their private myths. Mistletoe's movements had a jagged beauty, a style all of her own, fractured geometries of Dionysus. Lao combined flamenco, salsa, and African, surrendering himself to a compendium of dances. When they had run out of their personal repertoire they began making up new dances in spontaneous invention.

An electrifying energy gathered in the dancehall. Something strange was brewing. Everyone was soon carried away by the inspiration of the music and by the zeitgeist mood that descended on them. Happy thoughts in the music brightened the eyes of the dancers. They were all briefly magnetised by a new rebellion, and every part of their bodies smiled seductively. They danced themselves into signs and symbols, and celebrated the depth of mystery and joy in the body.

Mistletoe threw herself into a mountain body-song. Lao danced himself into a blue space in which he heard someone say:

You have to find the treasure or die. The clues are everywhere.

He spun around, and saw a six-pointed star on the wall. Everyone else was lost in their dance. Across the hall a stranger in a white suit smiled at him. Lao blinked, and the stranger was gone.

CHAPTER 6

Mistletoe was shouting something at him. He leant towards her.

'All we need is a clear sign,' she said loudly in his ears.

'For what?' he shouted back.

'Often we just don't know how to be.'

'What do you mean?'

'That's why people need gurus and icons.'

'For what?'

'To know how to be.'

They were shouting into the music and dancing at the same time. Lao could not entirely make out what she was saying but he felt she was speaking as if an important notion had occurred to her under the inspiration of the dance. She began saying something about how people are inducted into the zeitgeist when her face clouded over. An anxious look came over her.

Lao turned to see what she was staring at. In a corner of the hall the young man still knelt. He hadn't changed position since the afternoon. He had merely moved indoors.

CHAPTER 7

Mistletoe was upset that the young man had taken her remark to such an extreme. Such a thing had never happened to her before. She took Lao to a quiet corner and explained what had passed between her and the young man. She was careful to place the whole incident in the realm of youthful folly. She left it to Lao to dispense a solution.

'Send him on a quest,' Lao said after thinking for a moment and still breathing heavily from the exertion of the dance. 'That will transform him, and he's ready for it.'

'What kind of quest?'

'Give him something noble to do.'

'Like what?'

'Up to you.'

'Me?'

'Yes.'

'Why me?'

'You cast the spell on him. Use it now for his own good.'

'I didn't cast a spell on him.'

'Yes, you did.'

'No, I didn't.'

'You did. Why would he still be kneeling otherwise?'

Mistletoe was silent.

'Either you use that spell for his own good, or you have to be cruel to him. And I'd rather you weren't cruel.'

'Why do I have to have anything to do with him, for God's sake?'

'You already do.'

'I don't want to.'

'Why not?'

'Look at him. He's a small town kid who's bored. He's just looking for something to be obsessed about, to give his life meaning.'

'Then use that.'

'What do you mean?'

'Send him to find what he's looking for.'

'Like what?'

'I don't know.'

'You must have an idea.'

'All right. Send him to find the Grail.'

'The Holy Grail?'

'Why not?'

'No one goes looking for the Holy Grail nowadays.'

'Don't they?'

'It's not the Middle Ages, you know.'

'So much the better.'

'Why don't you do it?'

'Do what?'

'Send him on the quest for the Grail.'

'Me?'

'Yes.'

'I didn't cast the spell on him. You did.'

'I did no such thing.'

'The evidence is kneeling right over there.'

'He cast a spell on himself, using me.'

'Then use him to uncast the spell. Or use the spell for something good.'

Mistletoe paused, then she said:

'What do we even know about him anyway?'

'What do you mean?'

'He might have something to do with him whose name can't be mentioned.'

Lao scrutinised the kneeling young man again. Already people were gathering to look at him in puzzlement. Lao said:

'Even if that's the case, use it. Use the energy for something amazing.'

'Okay,' Mistletoe said. 'But you do it.'

'Why?'

'You seem to know what to do. You had the idea. The whole thing just irritates me.'

'But I didn't cast the spell.'

'In which case,' said Mistletoe, solemnly taking his hand, 'I give you the power of the spell and the right to use it.'

Lao, taken aback by her remark, gazed into her eyes.

'Okay, I accept,' he said, as if he too had been put under a spell.

CHAPTER 8

At that moment the young man caught sight of Mistletoe. His eyes lit up, and then dimmed. Lao indicated to him and he stood up and came over, many eyes following him as he walked. He stood before Lao and Mistletoe, pale and ardent, with a delirious passion in his eyes.

Lao looked deeply into the young man's eyes. He saw a fine pure soul, a confused young man waiting for the call. He saw idealism, sensibility, and suicidal thoughts. He recognised him as one of those rare youths who have once been spirit children and he was surprised to find him here in the west. He saw in his eyes the mark of one not entirely of this world, one who would have to make a great effort to accommodate himself to it. He felt sadness for the difficulties the young man would endure, and admiration for his eventual triumph.

'What's your name?'

'Nothung,' the young man said.

'Who gave you that name?'

'My father.'

'Do you know why?'

'No.'

Lao wanted to address the young man's soul in a language beyond words. He was thinking, we are made in freedom but live in our own prison. He was thinking, we are actors in a play. He was staring at Nothung, holding him fast with a penetrating gaze. Curious notions began to drop into Lao's mind. He found himself thinking about the silent watchers of the human drama who are fascinated by what each person chooses to become. He had the notion of being in the same drama, over and over again, actors in an infinite play.

'My name is Lao,' he said, 'and this is Mistletoe. We are on a journey to Arcadia. What do you seek?'

Nothung touched the pendants round his neck with nervous hands.

'I don't know.'

'But you are seeking something?'

'Yes.'

'You're a musician?'

'Yes.'

'And music is not what you seek?'

'No. I have music already,' Nothung said modestly.

Lao was about to speak, but Mistletoe touched his shoulder. She stepped forward and took Nothung's hands in hers, surprised by how cold they were, and she said, 'I want you to go find the Grail.'

'The Holy Grail?' the young man cried.

'Yes.'

'But where?'

'That's what you have to discover.'

'But I'm nobody, a simple musician, in a small town.'

Mistletoe was silent. Nothung looked at Lao for help. Lao shrugged.

'Everyone must find their own grail,' Lao said.

Nothung stood transfixed.

'This is what you must do,' Mistletoe commanded softly, 'or you will live on your knees, even if you are the king of the world.'

The young man blinked, as if he had just woken up.

'Then that is what I will do,' he said quietly.

He looked around, saw people he knew staring at them and, suddenly overcome with embarrassment, hurried out of the dancehall and into the dark.

CHAPTER 9

When the young man left, they tried to continue dancing, but inspiration had deserted them. The spirit of dance had gone.

Lao began to find the party raucous and the music displeasing. They had a drink, tried another dance, but all at once the music seemed out of tune with their mood. Deciding that their revels had ended, they went out instead into the warm breezy night.

They walked through dream-currents and enchantments. They walked through past and future time. They did not much notice the present. The lake quivered with dark-light. The mountain brooded, dark against dark. They lingered at the lake's edge, and listened to the wind in the mountains.

SECTION II

CHAPTER 1

That night, while they lay in bed, the spirit of the young man came between them. Lao could not get out of his mind the vision of the young man kneeling. He had looked the very image of a medieval knight. Mistletoe was calmly drifting off to sleep when Lao shook her. She was annoyed to be woken.

'What exactly happened between you and that chap?'

'That chap . . .?'

'Nothung, that was his name.'

'Nothing.'

'What do you mean nothing?'

'I mean nothing.'

'Something must have happened.'

'Nothing happened.'

'A man doesn't just fall to his knees like that.'

'Nothing.'

'On his knees like he was proposing to you.'

'Can I go back to sleep?'

'Something must have happened.'

'Nothing happened.'

'He was on his knees like he was prepared to do anything for you.'

'He fell to his knees himself.'

'You must have said something to him.'

'I told you. I said nothing.'

'You must have encouraged him in some way.'

'Why do you men always think that?'

'Think what?'

'That women encourage men.'

'I'm not saying always.'

'What are you saying then?'

'Come on, don't insult my intelligence. You must have said something to him.'

'I didn't.'

'There must have been an exchange.'

'Yes, he was bothering me and I was trying to get rid of him . . .'

'Not trying too hard, eh?'

'You're an idiot.'

'Don't call me an idiot.'

'I'm going back to sleep.'

'We have to deal with this.'

'I tell you the truth but you won't believe it.'

'The truth?'

'That nothing happened.'

'Are you saying he became obsessed with you just like that?'

'Yes.'

'What? He claps eyes on you and suddenly he's obsessed?'

'Yes.'

'You must have done something.'

'Like what?'

'Like look him in the eye.'

'In the eye?'

'Yes. In the eye.'

'What do you mean?'

'Did you make eye contact?'

'Eye contact?'

'Why do you keep repeating everything I say? It's annoying.'

'The questions are unbelievable, that's why. I can't believe you are asking me these things.'

'What things?'

'Like did I make eye contact.'

'Did you make eye contact?'

'Am I supposed to go round with my eyes shut?'

'I didn't say that.'

'That's the gist of what you're saying.'

'Nonsense. You're exaggerating.'

'Am I supposed to go round blindfolded, so I don't make eye contact?'

'I just asked if you made eye contact with this chap.'

'Eye contact with this chap?'

'You're doing it again.'

'Do you blame me?'

'You have something to hide.'

'I have nothing to hide,' yelled Mistletoe.

'You must, or why are you getting upset?'

'Upset?'

'Yes, upset.'

'Look, I was sleeping, and you wake me up and subject me to this grilling. Of course I'm upset.'

'So you're upset?'

'All this grilling, because of that chap?'

'All I asked was did you make eye contact?'

'Goodness, so I am being punished for making eye contact with every human being?'

'Don't avoid the question.'

'I'm not.'

'Did you talk to him?'

'Talk to him?'

'Yes.'

'He addressed me.'

'So you did talk?'

'Not really.'

'Either you did or you didn't.'

'It wasn't as straightforward as that.'

'I see.'

'What?'

'So there's something complicated between you then?'

'Of course not. You're twisting what I say.'

'No, I'm not.'

'You are.'

'It's quite clear something happened between you and you don't want to own up.'

'Nothing happened.'

'I think it did.'

'I tell you nothing happened.'

At that point Lao exploded. He accused Mistletoe

of inflaming the young man, of deviousness, of wanting to test her powers of seduction.

'I'm gone for one minute and you get up to all kinds of stuff,' he shouted.

The paradise of their room had turned into purgatory.

CHAPTER 2

At first Mistletoe retreated into silence. She turned a blank face to him, which exacerbated his mood. The more she withdrew, the more suspicious he became. The more suspicious he became, the angrier he was. He made coarse insinuations. He invented incriminating reasons to explain the young man's behaviour. He lashed her verbally, took advantage of her silence, and distorted what she said. He whipped himself into a fine fury. He was quite irrational. And yet he was oddly lucid, oddly aware of himself. Though he fumed, he really wanted her to do or say something that would free him of his rage.

Mistletoe made no reply to any of it. She bore his outrageous suggestions with a neutral silence. It was her way. Silence was her weapon. But then something he said, some allusion to the past, pierced her silence. Her face reddened. When she could bear his words no longer, she too exploded. Furious at being accused, angry at his blaming, she was soon too caught up in her emotions to see round the bends of her own rage.

They verbally flew at one another with all their

might. They screamed and cursed one another, faces contorting. They went at one another with a nameless fury, each seeming to hate the other more than anything in the world, inflamed with the passions of hell.

CHAPTER 3

Deeper and deeper into the maelstrom of their quarrel they descended till they were trapped in the labyrinths of an evil current. They went on hurting one another, wreaking vengeance, raking up the demons of past deeds, as if possessed.

They were unrelenting and unforgiving; but deep down they each wanted the other to say or do something that would turn the anger back into love. But neither wanted to be the first to give in. The shouting and quarrelling satisfied some raw hunger.

When they began to wish horrible deaths on each other, they passed beyond the boundaries of their personalities. They were no longer themselves. Some poison had insinuated itself into them. It was as if they were delirious actors in a play whose performances had taken them over completely.

Lao would stamp out of the hotel room, swearing never to come back, banging the door behind him. A few moments later he would return. Then a few minutes after that Mistletoe would storm out, and then come back. The quarrel would keep on beginning again and again, fuelled by their delirium.

CHAPTER 4

They swirled in this heart-heating inferno, hacking at one another. Their demons raged till ash-coloured dawn lit up the mountains and feathery daylight played on the surface of the lake.

Then something mysterious settled in them and they gradually became quieter. Their spirits stilled as they saw the sun rising over the mountain. Golden tints danced like little angels on the face of the lake.

Lao and Mistletoe had been awake all night. Soon they dropped off out of sheer exhaustion, like children who are lost and have fallen asleep in a garden; their faces were streaked with tears.

CHAPTER 5

That night a man with a bouquet of roses and a bottle of Dom Perignon slipped into Jute's room.

They talked about how they would sustain their love beyond the Arcadia journey. Then with a gasp and a sigh she received him, and eagerly took him into herself.

SECTION III

CHAPTER 1

In the morning, at breakfast, they had an encounter with Hans, the hotel owner, who was in a cheerful and expansive mood. He wore a cream-coloured suit and a blue tie and was clean-shaven, his moustache groomed. He was even friendly to Lao.

The other crew members had woken early and gone off on their different adventures. It was a day off from filming. Lao and Mistletoe were just finishing their breakfast of muesli and croissants when Hans joined them. Mistletoe had expressed an interest in the little town and Hans obliged them with its curious story. He was in a very good mood and addressed his story mainly to Mistletoe, with sliding glances at Lao.

'This town used to be very famous,' he said. 'The rich came here from all over the world. Goethe, Mark Twain, Hesse, they all fell in love with our mountains. Turner painted our sunsets. Princes, kings, tycoons, playboys, they all came to us in huge numbers. Then the others followed. They came in spring and summer and the town became immensely successful and rich. Once there were fabulous yachts on our lake with names like *Midas*, *Utopia*, and *Nefertiti*.'

'What happened?' asked Mistletoe.

Hans turned on her a kindly eye.

'They drank, they gambled away huge fortunes, they took drugs of all kinds. And there were the constant scandals. People committed suicide over failed investments, gambling debts, and women. It all became messy. The wheel of fortune turned, and everything went bad.'

Hans paused. He looked sadly out of the window at the mountain.

'The rich and famous destroyed us. They ruined our way of life. They corrupted our daughters, confused our sons, seduced our wives, made our menfolk restless and greedy. There were duels at night. People were regularly found dead in flower-beds. Others were found dead in their hotel suites, having shot themselves in the head, point-blank. One of them left a suicide note that read only: *Too little luck*. Another left a note saying: *I could have hung on, but it's too beautiful.* What on earth does that mean? This man was found hanging in the presidential suite of one of our finest hotels.'

Hans twirled his moustache thoughtfully.

'And so with fame, with money, with neuroses, they ruined the town. More people came than ever. It was like a stampede. The roads and lanes were crowded with cars. You couldn't move. There were beautiful women in furs everywhere,

284

money splashed all over the place, opera stars, screen idols, high society women, shipping magnates, they all flocked to our little town by the lake. Popularity, success, hysteria, killed us. Our town was written about in all the magazines and newspapers across the world. We were photographed to death. Our cemeteries became places for bizarre love-making. Our young men were paid to make love to the wives of rich old men, while the old men watched. Money became a plague, an epidemic, a curse. Hotel prices went up and up. The townspeople became greedy. We who had been like a large family, we fought and hated one another. Then something happened which changed everything.'

Hans paused again. He looked round the table and helped himself to a little coffee, taking a new cup. He had a few sips.

'One night,' he said, resuming his story, 'a young man of the town murdered one of the rich old men, whose wife he had made love to while the old man watched. The trouble was that the young man was madly in love with the wife. He murdered the old man with a knife, stabbing him twenty-two times in a crazy fit of humiliation, jealousy, and confusion. The woman of course didn't love him at all and she ran out of the hotel naked and screaming and the young man plunged the knife in his own heart and died instantly. It was the biggest scandal. It was in all the papers. After that the rich and famous stopped coming. They found somewhere else. The town fell silent overnight. Then it died. It became a ghost town. Many years passed and slowly the flowers started to grow again and freshness returned to the air.'

CHAPTER 2

While Hans was speaking, he seemed to change. His eyes were piercing. Lao and Mistletoe realised, almost at the same time, that he wasn't wearing his tortoiseshell glasses. They noticed also a curious alteration in his tone.

'Now we don't trust fame and publicity. We don't want noise or what people call success. We don't even want to be on the map but we can't stop it. We want to be our own secret. We want to be invisible, to show the tourists less than we are, to be more plain, more boring than we really are. Plain and boring is our camouflage against the curious, our protection. We make ourselves difficult to see. It's a kind of magic. Our lives are quiet and hidden. Only people who are looking for something special find us. We have retreated into myth. It's not surprising that you who seek Arcadia found your way here. Goethe would have approved.'

Hans gave them a sly look.

'Nothing here is what it seems. The town bends, changes, depending on who's looking. That's how it keeps its magic now. Enjoy your walk.'

CHAPTER 3

As they set off on their walk that afternoon, they took the opposite direction, walking away from the cemetery and along the water's edge. There were steamboats on the far side of the lake and gulls calling in the air. They hadn't gone far when they saw Jim, Sam, and Husk swimming in the sapphire blue waters. A moment later Riley and Propr stuck their heads out. They looked happy, their faces shining as they splashed and played about. They signalled to Lao and Mistletoe to come join them. Husk shouted something, and laughed, but the wind bore her words towards the mountains.

Lao remembered once seeing in an old book of alchemy a woodcut of a man and woman swimming in a lake of living water. The lake was not a normal lake and the water was supposed to be dissolving dark aspects in the archetypal couple. Lao thought of the woodcut now as he watched the others playing in the silvery water. They are swimming in an unknown element, he thought, and like fishes they will be hooked out and eaten by the universe, as holy food . . .

Lao and Mistletoe waved back at them, but went on into parts of the town they didn't know.

CHAPTER 4

They walked along a dusty road that seemed to be returning to its origins. The mountains looked like ancient gods.

The light seemed to bend things. Lao wasn't sure how.

In the distance, rising above the modest height of the houses, a church steeple pierced the sky. They walked in its general direction in silence. Then some spirit in the wind, full of odd notions, made them speak.

'We change from moment to moment,' said Lao. 'When we have the right balance, we're happy. When we don't, we're not.'

'Right balance of what?'

'Things of the body and things of the spirit.'

'Are they not essentially the same?'

'Yes, they are.'

'What's the difference then?'

'I don't know. Their frequency?'

'Like light and sound?'

'Something like that. Conversion of energies.'

'If that's the case,' said Mistletoe, 'then seeing is not necessarily believing.'

'Why do you say that?'

'It's what they depend on to fool us.'

'What?'

'That we believe what we see.'

'It's easier to fool people through their eyes.'

'But people only really believe what they see.'

'I know. It's a shame. There's much more to life than what we see.'

'Believing only what we see enshrines only what can be seen.'

'And so we don't question what we don't see.'

'But often we are brought down by the unseen.'

'I know. Anxiety, neurosis, stress, cancer.'

'By the time we see what they're doing to us it's almost too late.'

'We treat the seen symptoms, and die.'

'But the causes are unseen.'

'And because they are unseen we don't believe they exist.'

'There's something primitive about the phrase "seeing is believing", don't you think?' said Mistletoe.

'In a way,' Lao laughed. 'Some would say that a chair is a thought you can sit on, a perfume a thought you can smell, music a thought you can hear.'

'But that's playing with words. You won't pay for a shirt that's just a thought.'

'One might. The Emperor's new clothes and all.'

'Exactly.'

'So, what are you saying?'

'When we can see the unseen, hear the unspoken, that will be something amazing.'

'Science says we do.'

'With instruments, not unaided.'

'Some say we do it in our dreams.'

'But awake would be more wonderful.'

'Remember what Jung said?'

'Yes. *Who looks outside, dreams.*'

'*Who looks inside, awakens.*'

'Truth seems upside down.'

'And inside out.'

CHAPTER 5

They walked in silence. They walked through notions in the air. The little town glimmered. They passed houses with brightly painted balconies. They passed a white horse without a rider. About three minutes later, Mistletoe said:

'Did you see that tall man on the white horse?'

Lao said, 'No.'

'He was holding a riding crop.'

'Really?'

'And he was looking straight ahead.'

'That's not what I saw.'

'What did you see?'

'I saw a beautiful woman on a white horse.'

'Really?'

'She had long blonde hair that streamed in the wind.'

'Hair that streamed in the wind?'

'Yes. And she looked at us and smiled.'

'At us, or at you?'

'At us.'

'That's not what I saw.'

CHAPTER 6

They went on walking, keeping the mountains in sight. They had gone for a while in silence without any car passing them, when Lao said:

'That church doesn't seem to be getting any nearer.'

'I was just thinking that.'

'In fact, the longer we walk, the further away it seems.'

'Maybe it's a strange church.'

'All churches are a bit strange.'

'Maybe it's not a church at all.'

'What is it then?'

'A mirage?'

'Nonsense.'

'You are falling into seeing is believing.'

'No, I'm not. That church is real. I can see its spire.'

'It's a conjuration.'

'We're walking to it at an angle.'

'It's a sickness.'

'There is a perfectly straightforward mathematical explanation.'

'It's a cure.'

'A cure?'

'Something to do with vectors.'

'Ah, vectors,' said Lao, dreamily.

CHAPTER 7

A sudden breeze blew against them, whipping up the dust. There were figures in the dust, faintly seen but not seen. Then the wind dropped and the forms settled.

The heat was solid but gentle. Sunlight played on the wild roses along the roadside. They passed a vacant petrol station and empty hotels. There was a large billboard with faded images of yesteryear promising paradise. One signpost gave the distance to towns and villages. Another told them they had crossed a boundary. Beyond this was a thin faded ribbon of road that rode up into the sky.

They took a sharp right and suddenly found themselves in the concealed heart of the town. They went down streets of pretty houses. This was where the real life was lived. It was like stumbling into a quiet suburb on another planet.

The houses were like painted façades and everything was dream-like. Lao turned and saw, not too far away, the dazzling steeple of the church. They made for it.

CHAPTER 8

In the translucent light the church appeared to change colour and form. Cream coloured from a distance, they were amazed to find it muted blue as they got closer. From a distance it looked almost Gothic. Close up it was austere.

The church door, solid wood with metal studs, was shut. It was a plain and uninteresting-looking church with a boring little cemetery. The headstones were old and decrepit and colourless. Its dead were not interesting and had nothing to say for themselves. They who are normally so eloquent.

CHAPTER 9

Much later Lao and Mistletoe were to remember the visit to the church very differently. They were certain that in the environs of the church they had fascinating encounters with people they couldn't clearly recall.

Lao was to say much later that it was to a conversation with a caped man he met in the church doorway that he owed the transforming creative idea of his life. Mistletoe was to say later that it was while listening to a kindly old lady in a green shawl among the gravestones and acanthuses that she had the inspiration for the world famous series of paintings she called *Daughters of Pan*.

CHAPTER 10

But that afternoon, all they saw was a church whose architecture was unexceptional, its wooden door plain, its cemetery average, its paths overrun with weeds. There was nothing there to see but neglect and dereliction.

They had walked an interminable distance from the hotel, drawn by the church's spire, only to arrive and find nothing of any note whatsoever. The church was bolted and dead as though no one had worshipped in it for decades. And it was a Sunday.

Lao and Mistletoe were so disappointed that they went round the church three times. They felt cheated, their minds rendered empty by the emptiness of the church.

They were starting to leave when it occurred to Lao to knock on the door. He knocked three times, and waited.

The silence elongated time. Nothing stirred within.

CHAPTER 11

While they waited they stared at the curious cross-like patterns of the door's metal studs, and while gazing they fell into a gentle trance.

In that waiting, staring at the door, many things happened and they were not aware of them. Many excellent notions entered their minds that would bloom in the years to come. Many changes began in their hearts that would not be visible for a long time. Many dialogues took place that would alter the course of their destinies.

But they would never be able to trace the alteration of the unfolding years to that moment of empty-minded waiting, outside the door of the boring church.

They stood there, waiting for something to happen, when in fact everything was happening.

When they got no response from knocking on the door, they left.

SECTION IV

CHAPTER 1

Something made them look back after they had walked some distance. They saw that the church was now golden. Like certain paintings, like certain people, the church was more intriguing from a distance. It glimmered, as if it were smiling at a private joke.

The notion of a smiling building was a little disquieting.

They wandered down a charming street that ran through the interior of the town. Here, they thought, is where the real townsfolk live. Through the open windows they saw beautiful interiors, like film sets. They saw no one.

Without knowing it, they were happy as they wandered down the beautiful street, gazing at the spectacle of life lived in the mysterious town. They looked into the houses and saw televisions, aquariums, bird-cages, sofas, perfectly laid tables, impeccably made beds, paintings on the walls, bookshelves laden with books, mantelpieces, well-appointed kitchens, children's rooms with orderly arranged toys.

In the gardens they saw swings hanging from

trees, bicycles leaning on porches, treehouses, cars in driveways, lawns lovingly tended. Order and contentment radiated throughout and there was a fragrance of jasmine in the air.

CHAPTER 2

As they walked down the quiet street, Lao became aware of a presence behind him, following him like a shadow, sticking to the periphery of his sightline.

At first he thought he was imagining it. Every time he turned, it had vanished. But when he began walking again, it was there again.

He pretended not to notice this thing that kept effortlessly to the blind side of his vision. He went on, gazing serenely into the houses as if he were at a picture gallery.

The world seemed beautiful to him at that moment. The neatness of the houses giving an intimation of life lived in right measure. The rooms, the gardens, the perfectly trimmed hedges, all indicated lives without stress or anxiety. The houses and chalets were all different, in colour, in design, and yet they all complemented one another. There was an absence of regularity and yet the street gave them a sense of harmony.

After a while, Lao began to wonder what

this harmony might conceal. Could it not be achieved at the expense of creativity, at the expense, even, of humanity? It gave him a longing for wildness.

CHAPTER 3

They didn't speak as they walked. They did not encounter another human being, nor any animals. But they had just passed a garden with a magnificent oak tree, when Lao sensed that presence behind him again. It seemed to be hopping from one side of the street to the other, from one foot to the other, on tiptoes, in long elegant leaps.

Lao stopped and looked back. All was normal behind him. All was still. There were canna lilies, roses, elderflowers, hydrangeas, and long pink blooms in the garden; and the oak tree was solid, its trunk healthy and gleaming, its leaves barely stirring in the light breeze. The street stood bright and clean in the transfixing light of the sun. Nothing moved.

When he resumed walking, it was there again, stepping out of the air and only becoming real when he wasn't looking.

Lao breathed slowly, trying not to think, trying to act naturally so as not to awaken Mistletoe's suspicion. He stopped, looked around, and acted as if he were just making a detailed study of the singular unreality of the street.

But he couldn't shake the feeling that whatever was following him was intent on him. With long legs, it skipped diagonally, behind him, along the street.

CHAPTER 4

Then, as they walked, his mind became momentarily vacant, and Lao caught a glimpse of the Quylph out of the corner of his eyes. His heart beat faster. It was only a glimpse, but this time he saw it and remembered it from his dream on the train. He remembered exactly their exchange, and the somewhat sinister warning. Memory flooded him like an epiphany and for a moment he experienced an extraordinary expansion of being bordering on vertigo.

He tried to breathe normally and walked on, a little unsteadily. He swung a glance backwards. The Quylph was not there. He forgot all about it, and there it was. The Quylph, in its mischief, its perversity, seemed only to exist in Lao's oblique sight, his peripheral vision. Seeing it was not something he could will. He could not do it deliberately. When he tried, he failed. When he did not try, he succeeded. It was agonising. It was impossible. It was a challenge to the management of his mind. It gave him the curious notion that the best way to see is to not see. To unsee. And that in trying to see he only failed to see. Then he had an even stranger notion, that there is a whole world he was not seeing because he was looking; and that whole world, that vast reality, came into being when he was not looking, when he was not trying to see. It occurred to him that this might be true of doing too. This idea was so astonishing to him that for a moment darkness swam across his eyes.

CHAPTER 5

When he came back to himself, the world was re-established in greater splendour. Colours were clearer and more dazzling. The blue of a gable, the green of a garden gate, the yellow of a flower, the red of a hobbyhorse on an emerald lawn.

Lao glanced at Mistletoe and was glad she appeared to have noticed nothing. He resumed the adaptation of his mind to the arduous task of emptying it so that, without effort, he might see. But it proved more difficult than he wished.

Then he realised that when he looked straight ahead, at the houses, the flowerbeds, the rooftops, he saw the Quylph quite clearly, but in an indefinable way. When he tried to look into the periphery of his vision, the Quylph would slip further into that periphery. It was like one of those nimble childhood friends who hide behind you and keep frustrating your ability to see them.

The Quylph was long and thin and green. It moved on its two long legs like a cartoon creature. Was it a spy, a guardian figure sent to keep an eye on wandering strangers?

CHAPTER 6

Lao played a game with himself. He stopped suddenly, and the Quylph stopped too. It seemed to stop in mid-air, in mid-motion. Lao moved, and it moved too. There was no doubting it. He looked at Mistletoe. She had been looking at him, quizzically.

'Do you notice anything?' he said.

'Like what?'

'Anything unusual.'

'No.'

'Do you see anything unusual?'

'Not especially.'

Lao was silent.

'Why do you ask?'

'No reason,' Lao replied, walking on.

A feeling of wellbeing ran through him. He stared at the white houses and blue chalets and he gazed down lanes and little streets and he thought about their invisible stories. He noticed that the trees emerged from the earth so perfectly that they seemed like stage props. He admired the rooftops of the houses, and noticed the stained-glass quality of the air. Far away, the mountains loomed. There again was the diagonally skipping presence.

The Quylph followed them till they got to the end of the street. It was the most charming street they had ever walked down and they were moved by the open nature of the houses. That they had not seen any inhabitants did not strike them as curious till much later. The entire street might have been a façade, a projection, a waking dream, but this did not occur to them. The unreality of the street was what they took to be its beauty. They would be haunted by its solitary character for years to come.

CHAPTER 7

They got to the main road and walked in the direction of their hotel. As they went, Lao, without looking, noticed the Quylph standing at the end of the street, with a wistful forlorn air. When Lao turned, it was gone. Only a heat shimmer hung where it had been.

'A Quylph has been following us,' said Lao.

'Really?'

'Yes.'

'What is a Quylph?'

The answer dropped into Lao's mind a moment before he spoke. Later he would wonder where it came from

'It's a nature spirit, a guardian of treasures.'

'Are you making this up?'

'No.'

'And it followed us?'

'It followed us all the way down the street.'

'Why didn't you tell me?'

'I tried.'

'Is it bad to see it?'

'You're not supposed to see it.'

'Why not?'

The answer was whispered to him again.

'They're supposed to stay invisible.'

'And if you see one?'

'You're supposed to receive a message.'

'From who?'

'From the gods.'

They walked on in silence.

'How do you know about Quylphs?'

'They're a legend of this area.'

'And you saw one?'

'I wasn't trying to.'

'I'd have liked to have seen it,' said Mistletoe.

'I'd have liked that too.'

'Maybe everyone has their own Quylph that only they can see.'

'Maybe.'

Lao looked back wistfully. He missed the Quylph. He was glad to have seen it, and he missed the way he had to be in order to see it.

'You really did see a Quylph, didn't you?' Mistletoe asked.

'Yes,' he said. 'I did.'

SECTION V

CHAPTER 1

As they approached the lake, notions drifted through them like clouds over the mountains. The notions were sweeter in retrospect. Mistletoe was thinking how all sensations were filtered through the prism of feeling. Lao was thinking that humans are stained-glass beings, giving off the colours of their true selves in everything they do.

Mistletoe was studying the light refracted through the clouds. Streams of colour. All is conversion, and conversion is all, she thought. Light into colour, air into life, thought into substance. Conversion is all we do. We convert our birth into living, our living into dying, our being into love.

CHAPTER 2

The day had given the best that it could. They knew it, and they knew also that their interlude was over, their Arcadian days within their Arcadian journey. They now sought to bend the rest of the day to a lasting beauty.

They lingered on the shore of the lake, no longer looking at the mountains, the lake, the clouds. They let the mountains, sky, and lake act on them. They let go. They surrendered themselves, and vanished into the eternal present.

It's impossible to say how long they were gone. Mystics say a moment in eternity is a lifetime in history. It's possible that in the margins of their immersion is inscribed the history and future of the human race.

Such moments have no name. They leave no recollections in the mind. It's a moment's freedom made real and then forgotten: an angel's kiss that alters nothing except the total shape of one's destiny. Altered but not known.

CHAPTER 3

S tanding on the shore, they sensed a syllable streaming through all things. They heard the sustaining hum which seemed to originate in the depths of their hearts and in the farthest reaches of space. The hum washed through them and sweetened the taste of life.

CHAPTER 4

T hen they found themselves walking along the rim of the lake as if they finally understood it. They were walking and talking as if nothing had happened, but a moment of beauty had stolen into them to remind their hearts of their living rights.

They were light-headed with an unknown happiness. They felt the need to drink deep of that moment for all the unpredictable times to come.

Did they know it was one of those moments which endure longer than life itself? Did they dream of using these moments as a sword against despair? Did they sense that these moments were elixirs, life renewed in the laboratory of Arcadia?

They talked about dinner. Mistletoe fantasised about her favourite dessert, a rich chocolate cake, with cream; and Lao looked forward to a glass of Château Margaux. Then in that light-headed state they reminisced about funny moments on other shared journeys.

'Do you remember that train to Rome that we missed?' said Mistletoe.

'Do you remember that plane in Greece that had *Icarus* written on its side?'

'Do you remember that hotel in Biarritz where the owner wept all night?'

'Do you remember that train journey to Spain where the ticket-collector . . .'

'Stood frozen in the doorway, like the courtier in Velázquez's *Las Meninas* . . .? I do, I remember them all.'

'So do I.'

CHAPTER 5

Notions dim and strange danced around them in the air. Notions whispered to them from the grass, speaking to the soles of their feet. Things were whispered in their ears, leaving only the silence of the wind. Notions played within them like reflections on the lake.

At that moment Lao glimpsed a waterfall of clouds on a mountain peak; the light dying on the surface of the lake pierced Mistletoe's heart. It was such a rare moment that they couldn't help thinking how they could borrow its power against the darkness, or coax from it the art of living.

A pensive wind blew them back to the hotel. In their room time lengthened itself as day faded.

The clouds were wooing the mountain peaks. Mistletoe resumed her drawing. Lao began to write.

Lake of transformation

Living water burning with light
And living still it shines at night.

CHAPTER 6

While Mistletoe drew, she noticed a yellow boat on the lake. The light was perfect all around and brought out the richness of the yellow. Colour, at that moment, seemed to her a magical revelation of the garment of form.

She went on drawing. She made the mountain into a cake. She ate of the cake, and declared it good with a smile.

CHAPTER 7

Lao wrote another poem.

> *The Quylph*
> *Came from*
> *Aleph.*

CHAPTER 8

Beautiful days are all too short – pure music between the hammer beats of life.

The day darkened. It was time for dinner. They were all in a pensive mood, aware that their journey must continue and that many ideas they had about themselves must be surrendered. No one felt much like talking. They ate mostly in silence, and trooped up to bed.

Around midnight, unable to sleep, Lao and Mistletoe went downstairs to the lake's edge. The lake was dark and mysterious. They took their clothes off and stood naked. Then they slipped into the water. Lao could not swim, so he kept to the shallows. But under Mistletoe's coaxing he let himself submerge. The water was cold and dark and alive. With any luck, thought Lao as he rose to the surface, like fishes we will be hooked out and eaten by the universe, as holy food.

In that state, he was astounded to note that the earth was blue.

Little Venice
London
September 2013